I0684919

NOTHING FAMILIAR

SAM CHEEVER

ELECTRIC PROSE PUBLICATIONS

PRAISE FOR SAM CHEEVER

Sam Cheever creates some of the best characters you could ever find in the pages of a book.

Ms. Cheever writes with class, humor and lots of fun while weaving an excellent story.

Fighting powerful magical forces that threaten to upend her world, LeeAnn is alone and overwhelmed, and she's running out of time to save the ones she loves.

LeeAnn's life is taking a nasty turn. There are forces at work which are determined to expose the magic community to humans. One of LA's closest allies hovers on the edge of death. Grandmama Celeste has disappeared and, for the first time since LA's known her, isn't responding to pleas for help. To make things worse, LA's best friend, Deg, is attacked by Wraiths, and the healers aren't sure they can cure him.

LA soon finds herself on a journey to Underworld... traveling to Hades in search of a rare flower that's closely guarded by Wraiths. The journey is long—fraught with danger—and LA must trust someone who hasn't always been trustworthy for its success.

But her challenges haven't yet begun. Her world continues to burn.

Will LA be able to dispel the stigma of her own mistakes? Or will her friends pay the ultimate price as she gives herself over to the evil swirling around them all?

ONE

It hadn't been all that long ago since I discovered that Angels actually walked on Earth again. It had been an even shorter time since I'd seen the Angel standing before me last.

In that moment, I hoped it would become a whole lot longer before I saw him again.

"I thought this had been taken care of, Tollman," I asked him.

The angelic being dressed like a police detective glared down at me from a great height of six-feet-something.

In my mind, he'd always be well over seven feet tall. Not because of the kind of man he was; it was just that he got a lot bigger when he dropped the human mask and assumed his true form.

That kind of thing sticks in your mind.

Tollman shrugged broad shoulders, a glint entering one dark blue eye. "The spell to wipe memory only works on humans, Mapes. The Guild are apparently as immune to magic as they are adept at using it."

"But, The Guild are human," Deg argued, frowning.

Tollman looked down his perfect nose at Deg. "Do you know that for sure?"

My Witch's frown deepened. Nobody knew exactly what the Sensitives were. Though their auras appeared human, with a slight shading that reflected their use of magic, we still hadn't come up with an explanation for why magical energy could flow through their bodies without cooking them from the inside. "So, you think one of The Guild told this reporter...what's his name again?" Deg asked.

"Becksmart," Tollman growled out. He smoothed long fingers through his thick, mahogany hair and sighed. "Malice Becksmart."

"Quite a name," I murmured.

"Yes," Tollman agreed. His square, bristled jaw flexed with disgust. "And he definitely lives up to the *malice* part. We're all very lucky I'm the one he approached with this."

Shoving a long strand of wavy red hair behind my ear, I fixed him with a slightly hostile blue-green gaze. "Did he know about what happened in Town Square? Or just about magic in general?"

"Specifically, Town Square. But he seemed to believe magic use was running rampant in *Illusion City*. He implied humans were in danger."

Deg and I shared a look. There had been an incident in December in the center of town. Magic had been indiscriminately used against humans. We'd had to scurry to remove the memory of it from the human population's minds.

Up to that point, we'd thought the erasure spell had been one hundred percent successful.

"You wiped it from the reporter's mind?" Deg asked, his tone worried.

Nodding, Tollman leaned against the island in my cozy

kitchen and crossed muscular arms over his chest. As usual, despite the frigid outside temps, he'd rolled the sleeves of his dress shirt up to his elbows and wore only a dark, slightly rumpled pair of slacks with the shirt.

But the lived-in look of his clothing did nothing to diminish the almost visible energy flowing through his big body. The angelic being exuded strength and confidence, intelligence burning in his navy eyes. "That won't stop The Guild from telling someone else. Despite your warning, they seem determined to expose the magic-using community."

Deg shook his dark head. Like the Angel, my witchy partner was tall and good-looking, with black hair and intense silver eyes. Deg exuded an abundance of power too, but his was a totally different type of energy from the Angel's. As with all Witches and Familiars like me, Deg's power came from the earth—the elements—and was a light energy that left the world feeling cleaner with its use.

By contrast, Tollman's power was born of the Celestial environs. It was a foreign energy that rode the atmosphere of Earth like an oily film rather than filtering into it to become one cohesive entity.

During the weeks Deg and I had known him, Tollman had used his power sparingly. I figured the Angel knew his energy was too foreign for the Human Realm. Either that or he was trying to keep a low profile with the powers that be in the Celestial Sphere.

After all, we really didn't know why Tollman was living among humans. Or who he'd hacked off to be sent to us.

He'd been strangely tight-lipped about his presence on Earth.

"What do you want us to do?" Deg asked.

"Tell the council, for starters. The leaders of every

magic house should be aware of the dangers and take the necessary precautions. Then I need you to help me silence The Guild."

My head was already shaking. I didn't like the sound of that. "I won't be party to killing innocent humans, Tollman."

His handsome face folded into a disgusted frown. "I'm not talking about killing anyone, LeeAnn. But we need to find a way to muzzle them, or they're going to take all of us down."

Thinking of The Guild members I'd recently met, there was one in particular I'd suspect of going to the press with our secret. "I know someone we can speak to about it," I told Tollman.

He waited a beat for me to go on, but I held my tongue. I'd work with the Angel for the good of my people, but I didn't entirely trust him.

Mostly because he didn't even half trust me.

"I've already spoken to Littleton," Tollman told me. "He doesn't know anything."

Argold Littleton was a Dark Elf, and one of the wealthiest people in *Illusion City*. He was currently dating a Guild member and fully understood why they were dangerous...though he trusted them a bit too much for my taste. On the face of it, he would seem to be the perfect person to approach about our current problem. However, I'd learned one important thing during my last interaction with The Guild. They believed they were a cohesive unit. But I knew they had at least one member with a deadly agenda that wasn't good for the magic-using community. We'd busted that member, but I suspected he hadn't been alone in his ideology and goals.

"I'll keep you in the loop," I told him by way of a response.

Tollman held my gaze for a long moment before nodding. "Let me know if I can help."

WE CLIMBED into Deg's car because my little two-door, convertible sports car was death on snow, and I dialed one of our fellow council-members as Deg headed into the city. Brock was a Demon, a friend, and a good guy to have in our corner. He also worked at *Familiar, Inc.*, my family's company and ground zero for the magic-using population.

He answered his office phone on the fourth ring, sounding winded. "Talk."

I blinked. "Tough day?"

"You have no idea. The Trolls have destroyed the plumbing on the fifth floor, and the Fairies caught them using the facilities on their level. I've been picking Fairy feathers out of the ceiling tiles for an hour, and the ventilation system can't keep up with the explosion of Fairy dust."

Fairies tended to discharge Fairy dust when they were upset. It played havoc on people's sinuses.

"The sparkly stuff's spreading in clouds throughout the whole building. We all look like we have swine flu." He sneezed as if to emphasize the point. "War of the Realms has broken loose. Everyone seems to think I'm the guy to fix it."

"It sucks being a 'get 'er done' kind of guy," I teased.

He sighed. "When did I become such a grunt, LA?"

I fought a grin. "If I were you, I wouldn't use that particular word during the current situation."

"Har." The response held no humor, but I could see him grinning in my mind's eye.

"I've called to save you."

"Thank goodness. What's up?"

The smile died from my face as I remembered how dangerous our current problem was. "Tollman came to see Deg and me today. He says the magical mind-wipe from the Town Square fiasco didn't work quite as well as planned."

"That's bad, LA."

"Ya think?" I frowned, fighting to keep my temper in check. "Apparently, Sensitives are immune to memory-wipe magic."

"One of them talked?"

"Worse. Somebody went to a human reporter, and that reporter came to the police for a statement. Luckily, Tollman caught the case. He wiped the man's memory and sent him on his way."

"But The Guild's agenda still lives, and whoever told the reporter will probably do it again."

"Yeah. And this time they'll most likely make sure we don't get a chance to wipe it again."

"Okay, yeah, this is really bad. What do you need me to do?"

"Can you put people on all the news organizations? We need to know if anyone from The Guild shows up telling tales."

"Of course. But what do you want us to do if we catch one of them?"

"Bring him or her into *Familiar, Inc.* We need to figure out a way to diffuse this."

"Will do. Mandy's in the lab, working on some general use spells. I'll put her on finding something that will work on Sensitives. Just in case."

"Good plan. Thanks, Brock. Deg and I will be in the office in a couple of hours. When we get there, we'll fill you in on what we found."

"Where are you two going?"

I grimaced before I could stop myself. "We're headed into the eye of the hurricane."

TWO

The Guild had recently suffered a fire in their headquarters. The fire had been set by one of their own, and I hadn't paid enough attention to know if they'd rebuilt the organization afterward.

Apparently, they had. Unfortunately. Or fortunately, depending on perspective. I wasn't happy that they were still meeting and planning their foray into the world of magic, but at least we could keep an eye on their machinations, as long as they remained relatively out in the open.

Deg stopped his car underneath a railroad overpass, and we stared at the glass-fronted doors on the other side of a broken and weedy sidewalk. The doors were set into a blackened brick wall, just four concrete steps above ground level, with wrought iron railings that were covered in pigeon poop.

An elongated lump on the sidewalk in the shadow of the steps twitched just enough to tell me it was a homeless person, covered with a plastic tarp on the icy ground.

I frowned at the sight. "That's got to be cold."

Deg nodded. "I might be able to help." He climbed out

of the car and locked it as I followed. I stood looking up at the overpass, my mind still hearing the groan and rumble of the train that used to cross there.

I'd been sad when *Illusion City's* mayor had announced five years earlier that the train would no longer run.

Lack of interest apparently.

I figured it had been poorly run like most government entities. What we needed to get it up and running again was a private solution. Somebody with a bit of expendable cash and an entrepreneur's spirit needed to take it on and create a desirable passenger experience that would bring back the riders the *Illusion City* run once had.

Deg stopped a few feet away from the lumps—because as we got closer I realized there were several of them mashed together for warmth—and lifted his hands, sending the oddly twisted components of a spell into the air with his dancing fingertips.

From our work together, I recognized the remnants of a heating spell. Sure enough, the spell stretched with a soft whine as he completed it and then snapped back into shape, glowing red like burning coals. Deg sent it floating toward the group of homeless with a wiggle of his long fingers, and it settled over them, dropping down to wrap around the entire group like a blanket.

From within the cluster of mounded tarps, several long, happy sighs were the only sign of its effects.

I started toward the steps, a smile on my face. "Too bad The Guild can't learn to do things like that. Things that actually help somebody."

Deg frowned at my comment, no doubt remembering the last magic we'd encountered from the rogue Guild member.

None of it had been helpful in any way.

The steps were icy, and the glass doors were locked. I placed my hand over the lock and formed a mental image of the metal workings shifting inside. A moment later the lock disengaged with a soft but satisfying click.

I threw Deg a grin.

"Well done, Tadpole," he said, grinning back.

The door whined loudly when Deg pulled it open. We stopped, wincing at the sound. It was going to be hard to sneak up on them after that.

No sound met our jarring entry. Nothing moved through the vast, high-ceilinged space that had once been the public area of the old train station.

After a moment, Deg sent a *quietus* spell toward the door and let it close. He twisted his fingers in the air, and the deadbolt snicked back home.

No sense inviting innocent humans into the space. Just in case things turned ugly.

We walked softly, our hands stretched out in front of us, ready to respond with magic if necessary. I had a movement-squelching power word on my tongue to halt any shenanigans.

But none of our protective measures were necessary.

We rounded a wall that severed the public restrooms from the main space and found the man we were looking for standing there, his hands clasped before him and his icy-blue gaze locked unerringly on us. "Welcome to our new headquarters," the man said. I'd only met him once, but he'd made an impression on me that seemed out of proportion with his presence.

He was a small man, probably not much taller than five feet eight inches, with an abundance of dark silver hair and a mouth that looked like an anus when he was annoyed.

The eyes that watched us approach were a light blue, colder than the wintery day beyond the train station's walls.

I'd never learned his name during our previous interaction because The Guild apparently embraced anonymity. Or he believed, as Demons did, that names contained power and that you should never give your enemies power over you by sharing yours.

I noticed he didn't look surprised by our arrival. "You were expecting us?"

He inclined his head. "Mr. Littleton was kind enough to tell us he'd given you the address."

I would have expected irritation for the Dark Elf's interference.

I didn't see any.

"We told him it was of vital importance," Deg told the man.

He shrugged narrow shoulders. "The Guild has nothing to hide."

I seriously doubted the truth of that. "You know why we're here?"

He frowned. I thought I heard a soft sigh escape his lips. "Are we to be blamed now for every intrigue in the magical world?"

"No," I said. "But this instance seems to point directly to you."

"How so?" He tilted his head, the dim light high above him highlighting a half-dollar-sized bald spot amid the dark silver hair.

"It certainly doesn't benefit the magic-using community to be outed to the humans," Deg said.

"But we also are magic-users, correct?"

I opened my mouth to respond but wasn't sure what to

say, so I hesitated. What he said was strictly true. But there was a big difference.

"You're human," Deg said. "If magic is discovered, you won't be ostracized. You won't become the target of every anti-magic fascist in the world."

"You won't be hated and forced into hiding," I offered softly. I'd known all the things Deg was talking about, of course. But somehow they became more real to me in that moment. I realized how much danger I and my family and friends would be in. Our only choice would be to fight back or run. Violence would make everything worse. Especially when the human population realized how outgunned they were. Running would mean the end of everything we knew and loved. It would mean starting over somewhere else. *If* we could find a place where we could live in anonymity after we'd been exposed. "We want to co-exist with humans. We're tasked with protecting, not conquering."

His cold gaze sparked with some emotion. "You're so certain you could defeat us?"

His question created ice in my heart. Would humans find a way to win?

"We don't want to find out," Deg said. "Did you go to the reporter, Malice Becksmart? Did you tell him about magic?"

The man hesitated just long enough to create uncertainty. Then he smiled. "If I did, I wouldn't tell you. Now please leave. Don't return. You aren't welcome here."

"We'll leave," I told the man as anger sparked. I wasn't going to let a mean little man filled with hate and jealousy harm my family and friends. "But we'll be keeping a close eye on you. And, you might not think you want us as friends, but I promise you definitely don't want us as enemies."

I SAT in annoyed silence as Deg drove us away from the harsh winter landscape of downtown *Illusion City*. My mind spun with possible recourse for what The Guild was attempting. My anger made most of the recourse retributive. But I knew that once I cooled down I'd favor less drastic options.

If only we could come up with some.

"I think we should go see Angelica," Deg told me.

I flashed him a look. "Why?"

"She knows that guy. She can tell us if he poses a real threat or if he's just trying to cover for the person who does."

I thought about Deg's suggestion and finally nodded. "That makes sense. Should I call Littleton?"

"No need. Tollman just texted me her location. Apparently he's keeping an eye on her."

Dang Angel. How did he know they'd want to talk to her? "That was very perceptive of him."

Deg felt my gaze and turned, his handsome face mirroring my doubt. "Yeah. It was, wasn't it?"

"Am I the only one who found that meeting strange. I mean, aside from him basically threatening us?"

"He clearly knew we were coming. And he was alone. Where was the rest of the group? It's possible, if he's the one who told Malice, that he was working alone. That would make me feel better."

I nodded. If we only had one rogue Guild member to deal with, that would certainly be easier for us to handle. "Of course, he could be covering for the rest. Taking the heat, so they have more room to maneuver."

"A much more terrifying idea. But yes, I'd thought of that too."

"Our best chance of getting underneath this in time is to know who's behind it. We can't deal with an amorphous, shadowy presence lurking in the background waiting for us to screw up."

Deg's mouth tightened into a worried line. "For now we have to go with what's in front of us. We need to look into the leader's life, see who he knows and why he'd want to create the kind of havoc that outing the magic community would create."

I nodded. "Or how he'd benefit from it."

"Exactly."

"It would help if we knew who he was."

"You're right. And I know just the guy to ask."

TOLLMAN CLIMBED out of his beat-up wreck of a car as we pulled to the curb behind him. Watching us approach, he jerked his head toward the narrow, two-story brick home on a quiet residential street on the outskirts of *Illusion City*. "She's inside. She hasn't gone anywhere all day. Hasn't spoken to anyone on the phone. And my guys in the electrical surveillance department tell me she hasn't contacted anybody via email either."

I raised my brows. "Remind me never to get on your bad side, Tollman."

He shrugged. "She's either a bad guy or hanging around with one. Privacy becomes less of a 'thing' when that happens."

I shook my head. "Have you talked to her?"

"She denies knowing anything about Malice. She also claims nobody in her group would expose the magic community. She didn't come right out and say it, but

Angelica Gladstar implied she wouldn't harm her friends in high places by doing that."

When we'd met her before, the woman had been dating Argold Littleton, an influential member of the *Illusion City* community, as well as a powerful magic user himself. There was no question she'd be harming Argo if she outed magic. People would quickly assume his wealth was gained through unfair magical practices, and he'd become a huge target for jealous humans. Especially since he did have a lot of power in the city. He knew lots of people who got things done.

Still, I'd known people to do dumber things for personal gain. "Do you believe her?" I asked Tollman.

"Yeah. I do. But she might know more about it than she's letting on. That's why I thought it would be good for you two to talk to her. She might tell you more than she's willing to tell me."

"Because you're an Angel?" I asked with a grin. I was still working on getting used to that.

"No. Because I'm a cop."

"Oh. Yeah. There is that."

He snorted out a laugh. "Good luck. Let me know what you find out."

"Before you leave," Deg said. "We need to know the identity of the leader of The Guild. You don't happen to know that, do you?"

"Of course. I know who all of them are."

Deg nodded. "I figured you would have already checked them out."

"Just for clarification, I didn't get this information from human records." Tollman lifted a mahogany brow.

"Ah. Even better. So, who is he?"

"The name others know him by is Graham Cullpepper. But that's only his most recent alias."

"He has a past?" I asked, not entirely surprised.

"A very dark one. Let's just say that, no matter how this turns out, we don't want our fates to be in his hands. It won't end well for any of us."

"If you don't mind my asking," Deg started to say.

"I do." Tollman interrupted. "I probably shouldn't have even shared his name with you. I'm constrained from interfering in this realm. It's one of the key principles."

"Great." Deg nodded. "Well, at least we have his name. We can use our own sources to get what we need."

We headed toward Angelica's home. Behind us, Tollman's wreck of a car coughed and hiccupped a few times before the gears shifted amid a horrific screeching. He rumbled off, the engine ticking loudly. A cloud of black smoke and a horrible stench filled the air behind the car.

I grimaced, tucking a finger under my long-suffering nose. "You'd think a Celestial being could afford a better car."

Deg grinned down at me as he knocked on the Angelica's door. "You don't get it, do you? He's doing the hapless, bumbling detective shtick. The car's part of the act."

I chuckled. "Well, it's very effective. I thought he was a boob the first time he climbed out of that nightmare and walked over to us."

The door started to open.

Deg nodded. "Actually, I still think he's a boob. It has nothing to do with the car."

THREE

Angelica Gladstar was a curvy woman with dark hair and exotic turquoise-blue eyes. She carried herself with a grace and confidence tinged with arrogance that I was pretty sure was what had drawn the Dark Elf to her in the first place.

She looked down her long, straight nose and curled her lip when she opened her door to find us on her doorstep. "This is harassment."

Deg feigned shock. "Really? We haven't seen you in..." He looked at me. "LA, how long has it been since we last saw Angelica?"

"Weeks. It was right before Christmas, wasn't it?"

She rolled her eyes. "I know you're working with that cop."

I gave her a disbelieving look. "Really? When have you known us to work with humans?"

But her knowing grin told me I'd messed up. "I notice you didn't ask me *what* cop?"

Ugh! I shrugged, trying to look unconcerned.

"Don't bother denying it. I saw you talking to him out

on the street. What's your deal, anyway? The Guild had nothing to do with siccing that reporter on you."

"I think you're wrong," I told her. "We believe Graham Cullpepper was responsible. He all but admitted it. And we need your help to prove it."

Her expression went very still. She hid her reaction well, but the total absence of reaction was notable on its own. "Graham...who?"

"The leader of The Guild," I offered. Though I made it clear by my tone that I knew she was lying.

"Oh, you mean Gray?" She shook her head. "I know the guy comes off as kind of a jerk, but he doesn't want to blow up the city."

She must have seen the surprise on my face. "It would, you know. This kind of thing, especially after what happened at Christmas..."

"You see, Angelica," Deg cut in. "That's exactly the point, isn't it? Nobody should remember what happened. Yet you and the other Guild members apparently do. The pool of suspects is very small."

"You don't know that."

Something in the way she said it had my antennae rising. "What other explanation could there be?"

She started to step back, pulling the door closed. "That's your problem..."

Deg slammed a hand against the door, stopping it. "We can make it your problem really fast, Angelica. The whole group's problem, in fact. We've been playing nice because that's what we prefer. But if you force us to play hardball, we can definitely accommodate you."

She stared at him for a long moment and then shoved air out through her lips in an aggrieved sigh. "Look, all I know is that Littleton doesn't trust Malice. He says there's more to the guy than anyone knows. He's told me more than once to stay away from him. If I were trying to find the source of this problem, I'd look to Malice Becksmart first."

THE ARTIFICE GAZETTE covered *Illusion City* and about a fifty-mile surrounding radius, with minimal coverage of the wider world. I got the impression from reading the editorial section of the newspaper that the editors believed the rest of the world had been formed simply as a backdrop for *Illusion City*, and its importance was based only in how it reflected us within that framework.

The viewpoint seemed so entrenched, in fact, that I'd often wondered if it hadn't been born in magic. As if the original magic users who'd ventured into a pristine human realm decided they needed a vehicle for ensuring their small part of the territory stayed vital to the people lucky enough to inhabit it.

Deg held the front door for me and I slipped in under his arm, shivering belatedly as heat rushed in and embraced my icy form. "Oh, that feels so good," I murmured. He rubbed his hands together. I noticed they were purple from the cold. "Why aren't you wearing gloves?"

"It's not like we're hanging around outside throwing snowballs. We rush from the car inside and then back to the car again. Gloves are a nuisance."

"And yet your hands are the color of eggplant."

He jerked his head toward the long front desk, which bore the word "Information" across its serpentine front surface. "That's where we need to go."

I clutched a hastily assembled folder in my arms and followed Deg across the glossy black tile of the lobby area.

He stopped before a young woman with a diamond studded nose piercing and smiled. "Hello, I'm Deggart Kincaide." He motioned toward me. "This is LeeAnn Mapes. We're here to speak with Malice Becksmart."

She frowned at Deg and then transferred the scowl to me. "What is this about?"

"We'd like to discuss a possible breaking story with him," I said.

She shook her head. "If you'll tell me about the potential story, I'll point you toward the correct reporter."

Her dark, almost black gaze gleamed with hostility. I had to wonder why. Was it possible she recognized us? "That won't work." I leaned over the counter, lowering my voice as if sharing a confidence.

She shifted back in her chair.

"I was a confidential informant for Malice in a previous story. I trust him. I won't work with anybody else."

But the receptionist's determination was even greater than her hostility. "I'm sorry. Mr. Becksmart is our top reporter. He doesn't take every story that comes our way."

In other words, they wouldn't waste his time for a story they deemed unimportant.

"I see. Well..." I plastered a disappointed look on my face. "That's too bad." I shoved away from the counter and glanced at Deg. "Let's go."

Deg started to reach around me, and his hand bumped the folder I was holding. It flew out of my grip and hit the floor, papers flying everywhere.

A tinge of sulfur hit my nostrils as Deg murmured a power word only I could hear.

Disdo!

Paper flew up into the air, whirling above my head as if caught in a roiling wind, and several sheets hit the receptionist, falling to the surface of her desk. She looked down at the pictures, her eyes widening. "Oh, my."

She stood up and gathered the pictures quickly, handing them over the counter to Deg. "If you'll wait just a moment, I'll see if Mr. Becksmart is available to see you."

We watched her hurry away, disappearing through an unmarked door behind the desk.

"I hope Littleton doesn't mind that we made it look like he was handing the Mayor a wad of cash," Deg said with a little grin.

I shoved the paper back into our folder. "He's a team player. He'll roll with it when he finds out why we had to do it."

Deg's frown told me he wasn't as sure as I was about that. I didn't really blame him. As a general rule, it was never a good idea to irritate a multiple-hundred-year-old Dark Elf.

MALICE BECKSMART LOOKED down his long, crooked nose at us, his lips compressed into a thin line that seemed too wide for his narrow face. He wore his dirty brown hair so short on the sides the pinkish-white of his scalp showed through, leaving a pair of startlingly undersized ears stranded on the side of his long head like islands in a forgotten sea. For some inexplicable reason, he'd gelled the overlong strands at the top so that they stood almost straight up on his head.

The effect did little to make him appear serious or

thoughtful. But the arrogance shining in his smallish, light-brown eyes told me he didn't know or care.

As he settled his Ichabod-Crane-like form into a heavily taped faux-leather chair that creaked under his weight, the line of his lips ticked upward on one side to match the eyebrow he peaked. "I'm not sure how you people got past the bulldog at the front desk, but I feel like I should warn you...I'm very picky about what assignments I take on."

His gaze slid to the folder in my arms, and a predatory light filled his gaze. Despite his attempt to seem disinterested, it was clear to me he was more than a little interested in a potential hit piece on two of the city's most prominent people. "Why don't you show me what you have and I'll decide if it's interesting enough for me to write about."

Deg sat forward in his chair. "Mr. Becksmart, what do you know about a group called, The Guild?"

The reporter's gaze went icy for just a beat, lasting just long enough for me to wonder if I'd imagined it. "Never heard of them. Is that some kind of music group?"

Interesting response. If Becksmart really believed The Guild was a music group, he'd have dismissed the subject out of hand. He would consider himself far too important for the arts section.

"It's a secret group," I told him. "Their leader seems to embrace chaos. We believe they mean to cause trouble in *Illusion City*."

Becksmart's color rose just a notch, offset by the white line around his lips that told me he was pressing them more tightly together.

"Mr. Becksmart?" Deg prompted when the man didn't respond.

Finally, the reporter shook his head. "Never heard of

them." He stood. "Now, if you'll excuse me, I have *real* work to do."

"They were behind the devastating Christmas debacle at the Square," I said softly.

It was a risk. But a manageable one. If he didn't know about the magical chaos at the city's Town Square, he'd naturally be curious about it.

But if he *did* know...

Becksmart's long face formed into a neutral expression. "I have no idea..."

"You know as well as we do those kinds of theatrics could have been devastating for the city, Mr. Becksmart. The group is dangerous. We believe people should know about them and what they're capable of."

Anger added a flush to the reporter's face. *"They're* dangerous? I think you're focusing on the wrong actors here. The real danger comes from the *others*."

Deg frowned. "Others?"

"Of course. The anarchists who are really orchestrating chaos in the city. The people wielding the weapons of disorder. They're the ones you should be trying to point a finger at. Not the people trying to uncover them."

"Who are the anarchists?" I asked.

Becksmart ignored my question. He'd gotten his teeth into a subject he clearly relished. "The purveyors of power are at fault here. They're the ones fomenting trouble."

"Why do you think these people want to foment trouble?" Deg asked. I had to give him credit. He was sitting back in his chair, one leg crossed over the other, ankle at the knee, and his face a calm mask. He looked as if he were carrying on a rational, interesting conversation. Rather than fielding wild accusations from a spittle-flecked madman with bad hair and baby ears.

"Isn't that obvious?" Becksmart all but screamed. "Control."

"Control over what?" I asked.

His upper body bent across his desk in my direction. I barely held my ground. He jabbed a long, bony finger in my direction. "Over us. Over the normal people."

I felt my lungs tighten and suddenly found it hard to breathe. "Normal?" I asked in a slightly strangled voice. "What do you mean by that?"

As if suddenly realizing how crazy he was acting, Becksmart blinked, swallowed hard, and reached up to tug on one of the ears marooned above his neck. "The powerful will always try to control the great unwashed underneath them, Ms. Mapes. Since your mother owns one of the city's most successful businesses, I would think you'd understand that."

He frowned. "And speaking of successful, what exactly does your mother's company do, Ms. Mapes? It doesn't seem like anybody knows."

"Human Resources," I said quickly. "We provide temporary and permanent hires for organizations all over the state." I smiled my "business" smile. "I believe we've even placed people here at the paper."

Becksmart blinked hard and went pale. "Who?" he bellowed.

With a smile, I stood up. "Mr. Becksmart, if you decide you'd like to help us keep the city safe, please give me a call." I handed him the *Familiar, Inc.* card I just recently started carrying around so I could do what I'd just done. Writing my phone number on the back of a napkin or the label of a beer bottle just didn't say "trustworthy".

I felt his gaze on me as I turned and walked out of the cramped, overstuffed office. Deg joined me a beat later and we exchanged looks. Malice Becksmart definitely knew more than he should, which meant either he'd been in touch with our agitator again, or he himself had some magic. Either way, we had a problem.

If we added in the man's near manic state of mind, it became an even bigger problem.

FOUR

Brock strolled in our direction as we exited the newspaper. I'd forgotten until that moment that I'd asked him to keep an eye on the news outlets.

His darkly handsome face was filled with the kind of strain only an office job could cause. As he stopped in front of us, I noted the fine lines that had moved in between his eyes and the spark of sunlight off a single gray hair.

He was much too young to be going gray. Especially for a Demon. "Hey. How's it going?" I asked in a determinedly chipper voice.

He shrugged. "Mandy managed to create a spell to fix the problem."

I couldn't believe he'd delivered the news so matter-of-factly. "That's awesome! She can wipe the Sensitive's memories?"

He looked confused for a beat and then shook his head. "Not *that* problem. The Troll issue. She's magicked the plumbing..."

I held up a hand. "Stop right there. Any words you say

after *plumbing* are words I don't need or want...ever...to hear."

His smile was filled with enough devilment to make me wonder if he'd tweaked me on purpose. "You asked."

"No. I really didn't. What's going on out there in newsland? Any indication of leaking or inappropriate digging into our business?"

"Nothing specific. But we've been hearing a lot of buzz about some big story that's brewing. Becksmart's name keeps popping up, but they all seem to be speaking in riddles."

Deg sighed. "That can't be good. I doubt Becksmart is sitting on more than one story this big. The question is, how many of the buzzers know what he's about to reveal?"

I shook my head. "None of them."

Brock frowned in my direction. "How do you know that?"

"Because this is a bloodthirsty group. If they knew, they'd scoop him in a heartbeat. No way they'd sit on it and let him grab all the glory."

"Yeah, you're right," Deg agreed. "But it's still a problem. If they believe he's onto something big, they'll do everything they can to find out what it is."

"Agreed," Brock said. "I'll keep my people on this. If anybody gets too close, we'll snatch them up quietly and take them into the office."

"Keep us posted," I told him.

"Of course."

Deg and I drove in silence back toward my house. I couldn't shake the feeling that there was something I should be doing to keep The Guild from spilling our secrets and blowing up our world. There was one person we'd yet to speak to. And he was an important component of the current problem.

"I think we should talk to Littleton," Deg said.

I nodded. "You read my mind."

ARGOLD LITTLETON'S penthouse palace overlooked the rolling greenery of *Illusory Park* and the pond at its center. Unlike the last time Deg and I had visited, the landscape beyond the wall of glass didn't sparkle beneath a jewel-like array of multi-colored lights. But it still glittered under a thick blanket of snow, which I was beginning to think would never melt.

Argo offered Deg and me a hand, his dark gaze flashing. "It's nice to see you again, LA. Deg." I fought a shiver under the magical effects of the Elf's deep, melodic voice.

"It's nice to see you too, Argo. Did you have a nice Christmas?" We shared a secret smile. I'd discovered something about Argo at Christmastime that would forever change the way I looked at him.

"It was wonderful as always. You?"

"Perfect." My grin was filled with remembered pleasure. It *had* been perfect. Well...after it had been unspeakably ugly.

"What can I do for you today?" Argo asked. I noticed that, unlike last time, he didn't invite us in for tea and cookies. I was kind of sad about that. Along with a long list of other talents and accomplishments, Argo was a phenomenal baker.

I could still taste the buttery perfection of his frosted sugar cookies on my tongue. My mouth watered, and I was forced to swallow before I could respond.

Fortunately, Deg saved me from embarrassment. "We need to speak with you about The Guild again, I'm afraid."

Argo didn't quite wince, but his lips tightened slightly. "I don't know how much help I can be to you."

"I know you trust them, Argo..." I said, "and you're loyal to Angelica."

"No. It's not that. I'm afraid I've lost touch with the group." He spread his hands. "You see, Angelica and I are no longer together."

"Oh." I blinked in surprise. *Why hadn't she told us that when we'd talked to her?* "She didn't mention that."

He lifted dark eyebrows. "You spoke to her?"

"We did."

"What's happened?" Argo asked.

"It seems our memory wipe after the Town Square incident didn't fully take," I told him. "A reporter at the *Artifice Gazette* is threatening to break a big story about magic in our midst."

Argo paled. "If he or she is basing the story on that event, we can assume it won't be a flattering piece."

"Our thoughts exactly," Deg said. "It goes without saying that we need to stop him."

"Who is this reporter?"

"Malice Becksmart," I told Argo. "And we believe he might be a Sensitive."

Argo's eyes widened. "He's not part of The Guild."

"Are you sure?" Deg asked.

"I am. Before I entrusted knowledge of my lineage to Angelica, I insisted on meeting all of her associates."

"But they don't go by their real names," I said, frowning.

He gave me a look of such pity, I flushed. Of course, with his connections in both the human and magical worlds, he didn't need them to tell him their names.

"He might not be part of the group," Deg told the Elf, "but we're afraid he's working with Graham Cullpepper."

Argo sighed. "That's unfortunate. Becksmart's a nasty piece of work." He motioned toward the interior of the penthouse. "Come, sit down. This will require some discussion."

THERE WEREN'T any frosted sugar cookies, but the assortment of tiny, buttery pies was every bit as delicious as the cookies.

I sipped my tea and closed my eyes as flavor burst over my tongue. It was so delicious I almost forgot why we were there. A beat later, my host reminded me.

"I'm sure you've heard by now that Cullpepper is a dark and troublesome character."

I swallowed the bite of chocolate pie in my mouth and wiped my fingers on my napkin. "Tollman said something about that. Though he wouldn't give us any details," I added, pulling a face.

"Yes, the Angelic Code. Bothersome thing," Argo said. He frowned over his delicate china teacup. "Culpepper's a crook of the highest order. Always looking for an opportunity to put one over on someone. But his worst quality is by far the fact that he puts no value on human life." Argo settled his cup into its saucer. "When I learned he was a Sensitive, I tried to warn Angelica, but she doesn't see Cullpepper's evil core."

Despite having broken up with his Sensitive girlfriend, it was clear that Argo's inability to persuade her about Cullpepper still bothered him.

"Has he used magic for nefarious purposes in the past?" Deg asked.

"Most assuredly. Unfortunately, the fact that humans don't recognize magic for what it is works in the favor of the unscrupulous magic user. Cullpepper isn't one to reject that kind of gift. He's a master manipulator and a thief without a conscience. I can't prove it, but I'm fairly certain he's killed with magic."

Deg and I shared a look. "Do you think he could be manipulating Becksmart to cause trouble for the magic-using community?"

"That's highly likely. But only if there's something in it for him. You must be clear on one thing, LA. He does only what benefits him. Nothing less."

I stared at the last bite of my little pie, my appetite gone. "This is a mess."

"If you don't mind my asking, Argo," Deg said. "Why did you support The Guild if you knew a man like that was running it?"

"A fair question. I nearly didn't. Of course, Angelica pleaded with me to see things her way, but I was within a hair of going to the council with my concerns."

"I wish you had," I ventured quietly.

His lips tightened in sudden pique, but he nodded. "You have a right to feel that way. It probably would have been best after all. But in an attempt to be fair to Angelica and the others, whom I can assure you are generally a kind and hopeful bunch..."

I was pretty sure the people who'd been hurt in the Square would disagree with him on that assessment.

"...I took a different path to assure he stayed on the straight and narrow."

"What was that?" Deg asked.

"I have proof that he's used magic against someone from your house, Mr. Kincaide."

Deg's brows rose. "Really? Who?"

Argo's lips twitched. "The high priestess of your coven. The lovely and sweet-tempered Serena."

I choked on the tea I was sipping, spitting it across the space between us.

Argo lifted a flawlessly manicured eyebrow and dabbed at the front of his perfectly tailored navy-blue pinstriped suit with a napkin. "Are you all right, LA?"

I held up a hand, coughing violently. "I'll be fine," I eventually wheezed.

"He used magic against Serena?" Deg asked, his voice filled with disbelief.

Crossing his long legs, Argo sat back in his chair and grinned. "He did. To make things worse, it was a crime of a very personal nature. One which assured that his victim would never speak of it to others."

I felt my eyebrows climbing into my hairline. "Romantic?"

"Of a sort, yes. Suffice it to say, High Priestess Serena wasn't always quite so sour as she is today. I fear she's never quite gotten over it."

"But if she's aware..."

"She isn't. Not completely. She realizes she was played the fool. But she has no idea it was at the hands of a half-magic human."

"Jeezopete," Deg breathed. "If she knew..."

"Yes. They'd be naming a hurricane after her. Despite the fact that *Illusion City* is landlocked in the virtual center of the country."

I fought the urge to smile. I didn't like Serena. Pretty much nobody did. But it wasn't funny that she'd been hurt.

Deg didn't seem in the least amused. "Use of magic against a magic user is a capital offense. You should have gone to the council."

Argo's amusement slid away. Something dark skittered through his gaze. "I did attempt it. Serena begged me not to bring it forward. After much argument, I bowed to her wishes. But Cullpepper doesn't know that. He is fully aware of the consequences, however. Trust me when I tell you I've been monitoring him very closely."

I couldn't help thinking about the ancient symbols Deg and I had seen on the walls of the hidden passage at the first Guild headquarters. Before it had been burned to the ground. I had a strong suspicion the Elf sitting across from us might have had something to do with those.

My cell phone rang and I glanced at it. I recognized our resident Angel detective's number. "It's Tollman." I accepted the call. "Did somebody dial 911?"

He didn't give me the chuckle I expected. "LA, you and Deg need to return to the newspaper. Right now."

I frowned, glancing at Deg. "Why? What's up?"

"What's up is that Malice Becksmart is dead. And there are signs that magic was used to kill him."

FIVE

He was sitting at his desk, his eyes glassy and staring straight ahead. The reporter's hands were flat on the desk-top, the fingers splayed against the heavily marked-up blotter beneath them.

Becksmart sat rigidly upright, his legs slightly spread beneath his desk and his feet flat. He looked as if someone had braced him there so he wouldn't fall over.

A pale gray aura shimmered around him, sparking in the light filtering through the room's only window.

Tollman was standing before that window, tension clearly showing in his profile. He stared out at the filthy snow cover beyond the glass, hands shoved into the pockets of his untidy slacks. The window overlooked the newspaper parking lot, and the snow on the ground had been stained in the soot of a hundred cars coming and going throughout the day.

The Angel turned as Deg and I entered the office. He didn't speak. Instead, he crossed muscular arms over his button-down-shirt-clad chest and looked down his long nose at us.

The shirt of the day was light blue, wrinkled and unkempt as usual, tucked into charcoal slacks that had a rim of salty grime from the street along the cuffs.

"Tollman," Deg said as we moved into the room.

The detective nodded at my partner then slid his gaze to me. I wiggled my fingers, already moving toward the corpse in the chair.

"Do you think you can read his last minutes?" Tollman asked me.

I blinked in surprise. "How did you...?"

He shrugged. "I know a lot of things."

"Good," Deg said. "Then you don't need us. I'm sure you already know who did this."

"Hn," Tollman grunted. "I do have some good news. Unless it's masked really well, I don't think a magic user killed him. I mean, a natural born magic user. The signature of the magic is weak, diluted with human soul."

That was both comforting and concerning. If it was a magic user, I was sure I could pull his last moments from him. If he was killed by a Sensitive, I just wasn't sure.

Tollman unfolded his arms and walked toward me, stopping at the end of Becksmart's desk.

I caught his gaze. "No promises."

"Just give it a try, LA."

Taking a deep breath, I reached out and placed one of my hands over the dead reporter's hand, inwardly cringing at the cool, rubbery feel of his flesh.

I closed my eyes, drawing the energy that sizzled in my core into my fingers and allowing it to ease into Becksmart's flesh. I controlled the speed of its insertion, knowing that it would be easy to lose control if the energy waiting within the husk of his body was hostile or hungry.

I looked for a spark of life that I could grasp. It was

unusual for every bit of life energy to be evicted from the body immediately upon death. A small portion of magic usually remained for a while, a residual energy that I was able to tap into if I was lucky. That remainder was what I would use to read the deceased's final moments.

Unfortunately, I'd never tried to read a human soul. Because that was what the energy translated to in a human. What was a life force made of pure supernatural energy in a magic user, was something much more ethereal in a human. Something that went beyond magic and was tethered to the spiritual realm.

I had no idea if my energy could even meld with that insubstantial force, let alone pull something out of it. When nothing immediately happened, I increased the energy, sending my explorative tentacles deeper. I probed more meticulously in my search for that spark of remaining energy.

Rummaging around in there for several moments, I found nothing.

Then suddenly, something changed. I touched a spark, seeing an internal flare of light as the energy pulsed into life, contracting and drawing away from my foreign power.

I went very still, retracting the probing energy slightly so I didn't cause Becksmart's life force to retract again. I waited, expanding my sensors in an attempt to identify the tiny speck of energy. It was very different from what I was used to. Purer, less stark. Like a golden thread floating gently in a pool of mercury. I got the sense it would like to be set free. I needed to be very careful that I wasn't the vehicle it used to gain that freedom.

Aside from not knowing what residual effects that might have on me, I needed to read the energy before it fled the world for good.

A hand touched my shoulder. "LA, are you all right?"

I shook off Deg's touch, frowning. On the outside edge of my awareness, I knew I was breathing really hard, and that sweat trickled down between my shoulder blades, but I still felt as if I had some level of control.

That feeling didn't last very long.

The fearful speck of energy that had cowered away from my touch suddenly pulsed stronger and exploded into a painfully bright and burning essence. It flashed out and scorched my energy like fire, causing me to scream and pull away. But the energy followed, shooting toward me as I retreated, and I realized what it was doing.

Just before it would have ridden my magic into the ether, escaping me for good, I forced myself to stop retreating. Gritting my teeth against the agony to come, I wrapped the tentacles of my magic around Becksmart's life force and held on as it writhed and pulsed in an attempt to escape.

Its touch was pure torture, sizzling against my unprotected power and burning it away as fast as I could send more to hold it there. My throat hurt. On some level I was aware I was screaming, beyond the ability to hold it in.

Deg wrapped himself around me and added his energy to mine, reinforcing my hold of Becksmart's soul. He tensed against me and I heard his hiss of pain. But sharing the discomfort made it more bearable, and I slammed my lips shut on the screams that throbbed there.

I focused on reading the energy. Looking for a signature of the foreign power Tollman suspected had killed the reporter.

There was something hiding behind the painful brightness of the soul. Something darker and more familiar. I sensed its latent energy skulking there but couldn't get a proper read with all the interference between us.

I couldn't feel its essence or read the DNA of its magical makeup, but I felt its hostility like a low level hum behind Becksmart's soul. With a start, I realized the foreign magic was shoving the piece of human soul at me, trying to push me out.

Do you feel that? I asked Deg through our internal communication channel. I felt his nod in my head.

We need to get past the soul, he ground out, clearly in a lot of pain. I realized in that moment that he was taking on the brunt of it so I could do what I needed to do.

But I won't be able to read his last moments if I do that.

It's one or the other, he gasped in my head.

He was right. We could either try to see Becksmart's last moments, or we could attempt to identify his killer. It was a risk either way. With the reporter's soul doing such a good job of blocking, we could fail to uncover the deadly magic and lose everything. Or I could try to read his last moments and not be shown the killer. I couldn't script what I'd be shown. What was there was what I'd see.

I had to decide. And I had to do it fast. I could feel Deg's energy failing him more with every passing second.

Then the decision was ripped away. Becksmart's soul flared again, sizzling against our combined energy, and Deg screamed, the agony-filled sound like razors over my skin. My magic faltered and fell away, retreating so quickly I didn't have time to adjust as it shoved Deg and me so hard we flew backward and smashed up against the far wall.

"Tollman!" I screamed, as a pale yellow whisper of energy trickled from Becksmart's gaping lips and shot toward the ceiling.

To his credit, the Angel was quick on the draw. His hand shot out and he grabbed for the wisp of soul, wrapping one big hand around it and drawing it in.

The wisp of yellow mist sunk into his palm, and his skin glowed brightly beneath it. I pushed to my feet, my gaze locked on the Angel.

He stood very still, his eyes closed and his head back. The skin of his outstretched palm rolled beneath some kind of impossible force.

How could so much power be captured in such a small amount of energy?

Suddenly, Tollman's head snapped up and his eyes shot open. His fingers jerked straight, and his entire hand flashed a bright, silver aura, the energy snapping like a raging fire before extinguishing in a soft gasp of air.

I shoved hair out of my face and rubbed my back where I'd slammed into the wall. "Did you get anything?" I asked the Angel.

For a moment, he didn't seem to hear me, then his gaze slid slowly to mine. His eyes were glassy, and I knew he wasn't really seeing Deg and Me.

"Tollman?" Deg said, coming up beside me. "Are you okay?"

The Angel blinked. He looked at his hand and slowly squeezed the fingers closed before answering. "It was something dark. Ugly. But I couldn't get a signature."

His voice was soft, breathy. He stared at his hand as if whatever he'd experienced had affected him strongly.

"Was it human or magical?" I asked, feeling dread like a lump of clay in my belly.

His mahogany brows lowered. He unfurled his fingers and stared at the skin I'd watched shifting under Becksmart's soul energy a moment earlier.

He finally dropped the hand and jerked his gaze to us. "I have to go."

As he hurried past, I lifted a hand to stop him, but the

hand inexplicably missed, cutting through empty air. Before I had time to blink, Tollman was through the door and it had slammed closed behind him, causing me to jump under the violence of its closing.

I looked at Deg. "What just happened?"

He shook his head. "I have no idea. But whatever it was, I think it's a pretty good bet that it wasn't a positive development."

MY PHONE RANG as we were leaving the newspaper. I answered it without looking at the ID, my attention centered on the arrival of several police cars with lights and sirens blaring. "Yeah?"

"I need your help."

The police jumped out of their cruisers and ran toward the building, not even favoring us with a glance. An ambulance cruised up to the doors and stopped, sirens notably silent. "Who is this?"

"It's Littleton. I'm in trouble."

I glanced at Deg, lifting my brows. "What's wrong?"

"My name's all over the news. The police think I killed that reporter."

I looked at Deg. "We need to get to Littleton's." I spoke directly into the phone again. "Deg and I are on our way."

"I'm not at home."

"Okay," I said, sliding into Deg's car and shivering as my butt hit the icy seat. "Tell me where you are."

"I can't."

"Littleton, we can't help if we don't know what's going on."

"I didn't kill anybody."

"Then why do they think you did?"

"They received an anonymous tip."

I thought of Tollman. "Have you heard from the Angel?"

"He's the one who warned me they were coming."

Hearing the panic in his voice, I used a softer tone. "Argo, you know you can trust us. Tell me where you are. We want to help."

Silence met my request. Finally, he said, "I'm at The Guild headquarters. Don't bring anybody else."

I nodded to Deg. "We'll be there in five minutes."

Deg glanced my way as I disconnected. "Do you think that's what Tollman saw when he read Becksmart's soul energy?"

I frowned. "It sure looks that way. But since the Angel won't talk to us, who the heck knows? He did call to warn Littleton though, so I doubt he believes he's the culprit."

Deg shook his head. "What a mess."

"Yeah."

The radio played an energetic new song by a group called *The Imposters*. I reached to turn it down. My nerves were jangled and I needed some quiet to think. But, as my fingers found the volume, the music was cut off and a frantic voice came on air. "This is an emergency. Please don't turn away from this station."

I heard genuine panic in the voice. It stopped me in mid-action.

"We've just been informed that Malice Becksmart, Reporter for *The Artifice Gazette* was murdered. Sources tell us his death is tied to events that occurred in a recent attack at Town Square."

I felt my eyes go wide. Deg slowed the car, his gaze sliding to mine.

"Becksmart was working on a huge story our sources tell us was part of a massive cover-up by generally unknown persons. What we do know—and it's vital that you listen carefully—is that there are those among us who have...for the lack of a better word...powers, which give them the ability to use deadly force against the rest of us. We are all in danger! The Mayor has declared a state of emergency in *Illusion City*. No one is allowed on the streets. I repeat. No one is allowed outside. Lock yourselves inside and wait for further instructions. If you're caught on the streets, you'll be arrested. Heaven help us all people. I think we've been infiltrated by aliens!"

SIX

Deg slowed to a stop and sat staring straight ahead. I made a soft sound of alarm, my breathing stuttering due to panic.

It appeared Littleton hadn't been wrong about the danger of humans discovering magic. Except that the scope of the problem was much bigger than even he'd thought. One of our own had already been targeted. "What are we going to do?" I asked Deg.

Deg shook his head, his hands tightening on the steering wheel until it creaked under the pressure. "The council."

Yes. He was right. The council needed to meet immediately to discuss how to proceed. We had to get whatever was brewing under wraps.

As if on cue, both of our phones started to ring. Moving as if under water from shock, Deg and I pulled out our phones and hit *Answer* without looking at the number.

"Uh huh," I mumbled, still in shock. There was a pause on the other end of the line, during which I was dimly aware of Deg talking in a dazed tone.

"LA?"

I mentally shook off the fear that had me wrapped in a haze of ice. "Yeah. It's me, Mother."

"You heard?"

I nodded, then realized she couldn't hear me and spoke. "Yes."

"This is bad, LeeAnn."

I frowned, hearing the censure in her voice. "I'm well aware, Mother. Deg and I are in shock."

She sighed. "We are too. But we don't have time for that. We need a game plan. I want the two of you back here immediately."

I started to tell her we'd be there, then realized I couldn't do that. "We can't. Littleton's in trouble. We're heading there now."

"This is bigger than one Elf, LA." She was using her stern, queenly tone, and my gut reaction was to buckle to it, as I'd done with Grandmama Celeste for years. Instead, I shook my head. "This isn't about choosing sides, Mother. Littleton's been isolated as the one behind Becksmart's murder. If he's taken in and they get even an inkling of what he is..."

Her silence told me she understood my concern. "Argold's been dealing with humans for centuries. He'll handle it. And we have the Angel on the inside to help him."

I frowned, remembering how Tollman had run from the scene of the crime. "I'm not sure Tollman's going to be much help. He seems to have his own agenda."

"Come back to the office now, LA. That's an order."

The connection ended in my ear. I sat there for a moment, listening to Deg trying to get off his own call. He hung up a moment later and turned to me, frowning. "High Priestess Serena being her usual sweet and friendly self."

He rubbed a hand over his face, not managing to wipe away the scowl. "I'm assuming your call was as unpleasant as mine?"

I nodded. "That was my mother."

"What did she say?"

"She ordered us back to *Familiar, Inc.*"

"How soon?"

"Now. She said Argo was on his own."

Deg nodded. "Serena said much the same." He put the car into gear and pulled away from the curb, continuing the way we'd been going. "We're five minutes from Guild headquarters."

I smiled over the fact that he and I were on the same page. "Good. I didn't like the way Littleton sounded. The sooner we get there, the better."

THE STREET outside the entrance to Guild headquarters was empty. The wind soughed through the space, tugging up the corners of a discarded plastic drop cloth that I was pretty sure had been covering a homeless person the last time we'd been there.

The plastic wrapped itself around a light pole, billowing softly in the middle as the foul-smelling breeze danced through the underpass formed by the old, brick carcass of the defunct train station.

I'd expected that I'd need to magic the lock again, but the knob turned easily in my hand. As soon as we stepped through, the door was ripped from my grip and slammed closed, all three deadbolt locks sliding home.

Deg and I shared a look. Littleton had put a spell on the door that was targeted directly to us.

Like before, the place was quiet and mostly dark. Even the big room where we'd confronted Graham Cullpepper was dark, except for a weak light coming in through the filthy stained glass dome high above our heads.

I expected to see Littleton standing in the high-ceilinged main room that had been the public area for the train station. He wasn't there.

Just in case the unexpected happened, we gathered power, holding it just beneath our skin as we moved through the defunct train station.

Walking softly because we weren't sure what to expect, we didn't call out to the Elf. We didn't want to draw attention to ourselves. The fact that he hadn't been waiting for us was disconcerting.

After several moments of not finding him, I looked at Deg. "He's gone."

"Can't be. He left us the magic key. He's here somewhere."

My gaze slid around the big room again and landed on the dark hallway across from the entrance. We'd been down there once but hadn't searched every inch of every room. "I guess we'll need to look more carefully," I told Deg.

He nodded. "I'll check the old restaurant again."

"I'll look down this hallway and the offices."

The hall, which contained the restrooms and a janitor's closet, was cut off from everything else by a long wall, making it dark as pitch. As soon as I stepped into the passageway, the remnants of a sulfurous smell made my nose twitch with the need to sneeze. Sulfur meant magic, and in a place like The Guild headquarters, which generally housed only Sensitives whose use of magic was unnatural and inherently dangerous, encountering evidence that magic had recently been used was bad.

Littleton wasn't in either of the restrooms or the closet. I returned to the main room and was about to follow Deg into the huge restaurant space when I saw a muted glow coming from the train tracks.

It flickered like flame but sent an oily, sulfurous stench into the train station. Whatever it was, I knew it wasn't good. And Littleton was very likely in danger.

"Deg!" I took off running without waiting for him to join me, trusting him to follow as I plunged into the shadowed, refuse-strewn space.

I jumped off the platform onto the abandoned train tracks and something small and furry skittered away from me with a shriek. I dodged away from it with my own squeal and then, embarrassed, took off running toward the distant glow. As I ran, my feet crunched down on a thick layer of litter, which consisted of discarded fast food wrappers, old newspapers, and other things best left unexamined.

The light was coming from an abandoned train car a block or so down the tracks. As an icy breeze slipped past, I wondered how The Guild members had closed off the area to secure it. From what I remembered, the train cavern had once been open on both ends to accommodate the train's passage through the station. I thought the city might have bricked it up when the station was closed down, but the icy breeze made me wonder if there was still an opening somewhere.

To my horror, I saw that the illumination ahead was growing. What I'd first believed was a simple magical aura, was actually a supernaturally-induced conflagration. As I approached, flames licked from the broken car windows, crawling over the roof and down the sides like oil from a boiling caldron.

Black, sulfurous smoke billowed from the burning train

car and spread until I was sucking the poisonous stuff into my lungs with every breath I took.

I was forced to slow down, spinning a cloaking web that would cover my face and allow me to breathe through the miasma. *Deg! Hurry. Something's really wrong.*

He didn't respond, but I didn't have time to consider why. Something dark and boneless had climbed from the windows, right through the fire.

And it was staring at me through glowing orange eyes.

SEVEN

I screeched to a halt, my chest heaving from the exertion of running the length of the tracks, and watched with a horrified gaze as several more of the things slid from the car. I counted a dozen before I stopped counting and started looking for escape options.

It was a trap!

I shook my head even as I had the thought, mad at myself for being so completely drawn into it. I watched them.

They watched me.

Something about them was familiar. Though I was far too agitated at the moment to remember where I'd seen them before.

Or what they were.

The creatures started toward me and I stepped back, my hands coming up and magic sputtering from my fingertips. "Stay back!"

They didn't even hesitate. In fact, they seemed to move more quickly in my direction. I gathered enough energy to exterminate a room full of Demons and flung it at them, expecting to see them burst into tiny pieces of supernatural ugliness.

They bowed backward when my magic hit them, their shadowy, amorphous shapes bulging outward as the energy hit, and their limbs jerking with the force. The light from my magic flared when it touched them, and then slowly dimmed, seeming to sink beneath their black, lifeless skin.

Instead of exploding into pieces, they seemed energized by my attack. Their eyes glowed brighter as they started forward again.

It was as if they'd absorbed my energy. Like it had made them stronger. The nearest one threw back its head, emitting an ear-splitting shriek that made me cringe away with a cry, covering my ears in self-defense. I saw movement out of the corner of my eye and jerked my head up. The center of the leader's spider-like form split apart in about a ten-inch vertical slash and a thick, silvery mist sprayed toward me from the breach.

I barely slammed up a protective web before the spray bathed me in foul-smelling magic. It sizzled against my web like acid, eating holes through my energy as I watched.

Horror filled my chest. I started to back away, more energy sputtering at my fingertips, even though I knew I couldn't use it against them.

It would only make them stronger.

The creatures became more agitated as the magic leached from under my skin, merging together into a vibrating pack and surging forward as if they were drawn helplessly toward the power.

At a loss for anything else to do, I turned and started to run.

A bitter breeze shot down the concrete tunnel, bathing

my back and legs in sulfurous stink. I stumbled as it burned my skin, leaving behind a film of ice.

My teeth clacked together from the sheer force of the cold, and it was all I could do to keep running as it hit me.

Deg! I shrieked in my mind as I stumbled forward. *Where are you?*

His silence was more ominous than the raspy breath of the things who rode my heels down the track. Something was very wrong.

First Littleton and then Deg.

Whatever was going on, if I was going to help them, I couldn't be next. I reached the wide archway leading to the station but couldn't stop. If I slowed enough to climb back up onto the platform, they'd be on me before I managed to reach the top.

With every stride I took, they covered an area twice what I could. I was seconds away from being overrun.

There was no doubt in my mind that I would die if they touched me.

I ran on, praying I'd been right earlier, and there was an opening of some sort on the other end. The chill riding me from behind was unlike any cold I'd ever experienced. It stiffened my limbs, coating my skin with ice. Stumbling with nearly every step, I realized with a rush of fresh fear that was their game. They hoped to make me so cold my legs and feet would stop working.

I gritted my teeth against the growing numbness leaching through my legs and staggered onward. A clawed hand found my shoulder, closing over it like an icy vise, and I screamed as dark images shot through my mind.

Images of fear and violence, death and gore. In sheer desperation, I screamed a power word, "*Expellus!*"

The thing jerked slightly, losing its grip on my shoulder.

But even under the maximum energy inherent in a power word, it only flew backward a few inches.

It was enough to buy me time though, and I took it.

As I ran, my fingers worked on the air in front of me, crafting a warming spell infused with protective magics.

I couldn't use offensive energy against the things. I only hoped they couldn't suck energy from my defensive power.

I made the final slash of magic on the air to close the spell and heard it snap into place around me, snugging over my body and spreading warmth on magic fingers through my chilled and numbed flesh.

It was such a relief I almost stopped running. But I wasn't willing to test the efficacy of my spell. Not against something that clearly came from the wrong side of Hell's tracks.

Then it hit me. I stumbled again as I had the clarifying thought.

I needed to fight hellfire with hellfire. *Celeste!* Technically my grandmama wasn't residing in Hell, but she'd been known to make use of its inhabitants as spiritual Uber-style transportation when necessary. *Grandmama! I need your help. Now!*

A shadow shot past me. Then another, followed by a third. I recognized the tactic. They were trying to surround and cut me off. I was running out of options. I shivered as their blustery auras encircled me and prayed my spell would hold.

Celeste!

Calm yourself, girl. What's all the hollering about?

Her voice in my mind soothed me enough to allow me to breathe past the tightening of fear in my chest. *I'm under attack. I think these things are some kind of Wraith. They seem to be able to absorb and use my energy. How do I stop them?*

Describe them to me. Her voice no longer held impatience. Instead, it throbbed with tension.

Like elongated shadows, vaguely man-shaped. Long fingers with claws. One of them sprayed something like acid at me.

Eyes?

Glowing and orange. Like fire. They actually came from fire at first, but they're cold enough to freeze the warts off a Dark Witch.

No.

I didn't like the sound of her response. Or the sound of the taut silence that followed. *Celeste?*

She sighed. *Wraiths from the Tenth circle of Hell. They can call fire and ice. They're impervious to nearly all kinds of magic.*

I screeched to a halt as two more Wraiths leaped ahead and watched with horror as they tightened the circle they'd formed around me. *So how do I kick their ugly butts?*

You don't. They answer only to their master. Once they've been sent after someone, they don't stop until they've killed their target.

Her voice was soft, filled with sorrow. As if I were already dead.

You're telling me someone sent them after me?

I doubt it. If they had, you'd already be dead. My guess is you stumbled upon them devouring their actual target and they're not sure what to do with you.

Then they'll probably go away? I asked hopefully.

Unlikely. Can you tell which one is the leader?

I cast my gaze around the circle, energy spitting on my fingers just in case I needed to buy myself a few seconds.

They all look exactly the same. No. Wait. One of them is slightly bigger. His eyes are a darker orange.

Okay, that's the one you want. You need to touch him, LA. You need to use your tracking energy to find the person commanding him. Stopping that person will stop the Wraiths.

Oh, hard no! I shouted back.

Trust your protective magics, girl. You can do this. I'll stay with you and help if I can.

Every instinct inside me screamed that I should start running and not look back. But even if the Wraiths weren't really after me, I doubted they'd just let me leave.

Another thought occurred. If the Wraiths had been sent to get Littleton, I needed to know who'd sent them. There was a very good chance that whoever had targeted Littleton had also killed Malice Becksmart.

Okay. How do I do this?

You're not going to like it.

I already don't.

Okay. When I tell you to, look into the eyes of the Wraith you believe is the leader. Not now! Wait until I tell you the rest.

I'm waiting, I snapped.

You need to pull your tracking energy forward. You'll have to move fast once you have him because he'll use fire and ice against you. Do you understand?

Tracking energy, stat. Got it.

Why don't I feel like you're taking this seriously?

I'm as serious as a Demon with boils. Now, get on with it, please. The natives are getting restless.

Okay, as soon as you touch him, send the energy into him.

Does it matter where?

What?

What part of his body do I send it into?

If you can access his mouth that would be best.

Okay... I peered at the thing directly across from me. The circle had tightened until he was only ten feet away. Arctic cold pressed against my protective barrier, some of it leaking through to turn my skin to ice.

Where exactly is the mouth?

That's where the acid came from, girl. Pay attention!

Ugh! It's in the middle of his body. That's just wrong.

I didn't design them, LA. Now listen. If you neutralize him, you neutralize all of them.

Good. I'd hate to have to do this a dozen times.

Silence pulsed between us. When she spoke, her tone was uncertain. *There are twelve of them?*

Yeah. Is that significant?

She hesitated. *I'm coming to help.*

But the circle had tightened again as I blinked. *There's no time. Just tell me...*

Without warning, the slit that apparently served as the lead Wraith's mouth opened and the eardrum-shattering sound razored through my brain again, along with a wide spray of the nasty acid.

Wraith spit. Ugh!

My knees buckled under the agony of the shrill tones. I hit the rusty metal of the tracks and fell backward, curling into a fetal position. I pressed my hands over my ears and screamed from the pain. Warm moisture trickled from my ears.

I pulled my hands away and saw blood. *He's tearing my head up from the inside!* I screamed to Celeste.

Look into his eyes, LA. Hurry!

I forced my gaze to the Wraith's and, faster than I could

blink, the thing shot across the space, slamming into me and pinning me to the filthy gravel between the tracks.

My head slammed back into the rocks as an agony-filled shriek left my lungs. Pain seared through me the entire length of my body. Everywhere the thing touched me felt as if it was burning and freezing at the same time. It was the most excruciating pain I'd ever felt, and my mind felt as if it was melting beneath it.

Beyond the screaming and the agony, I heard a shrill, familiar voice calling my name. But I no longer cared. I just wanted the pain to be over. I wanted the thing riding me in that dank, horrible place to end it all.

I wanted to die.

The world behind the Wraith boiled black and slammed into the creature, knocking it half off me.

Now, LA! My grandmama's voice roared. It was her Queen-of-the-Familiars voice. An order. Not a request.

I reacted on sheer instinct, slamming a palm into the moist, disgusting slit at the center of the Wraith's shadow-like body. I bit back a cry of discomfort as my skin burned and smoked in contact with the acidic contents.

Gritting my teeth, I sent my tracking energy into the creature, closing my eyes as the power cut a path directly to the core of the thing's magic, deep inside its black aura. I turned my magic into claws and slashed my way through, not caring if I caused it damage or agony. That was the least it deserved after the pain it had caused me.

I was vaguely aware of its screams. But I was internally focused, my power reading the paths of its energy like a road map. I sliced through a black lump of flesh and light speared out. The illumination was orange and flickered like fire.

I quickly wrapped my energy around it before it could

skitter away, turning up the power to hold it in place while I inserted a fine strand of my tracking magic.

The needle of my special power hit the flickering orange light and sparks flared outward, melting the energy holding it in place.

I doubled down on my efforts to keep it there. Beyond the oily black world I'd immersed myself in, the sounds of battle filtered through, the echo of screams and the stench of sulfurous energy making the ground beneath me quake.

I found what I was looking for a beat later. A small shadow of silvery light that clung to the edges of the Wraith's foul energy, hiding in the flare from its aura. I magically sniffed the foreign energy, trying to identify its source, but it was unlike anything I'd ever seen before.

Unfortunately, the Wraith's aura was masking it.

If only I could peel it free...isolate it...maybe I could read the signature within the snippet of residual power.

But as I reached for the tiny invader, the Wraith suddenly screamed again. Something inside my head popped and misery flared through my mind.

Before I realized what I'd done, I'd yanked my magic free and thrown myself to the ground. I just had time to cover my head with my arms before the thing rose up into the air and burst, spraying oily black gore and burning spit over me and everything nearby.

EIGHT

"LA?"

The voice was muffled as if covered in a hundred blankets. I just lay there for a moment, hoping that if I didn't move, no more of the Wraiths would descend on me.

"LA!"

Celeste's voice had gotten bossier. I frowned. And deeper? A big hand shoved against my shoulder, and I finally realized it wasn't my grandmama who was yelling at me. My eyes popped open and I found myself looking into Brock's dark, worried face. I was startled to see that he'd taken his Demon form.

"Are you okay?"

I could see his lips moving but I could just barely hear him. Then I remembered the popping sound inside my head. I pointed to my ears. "I think my eardrums burst." Even my own voice sounded strange to me. I reached up and touched the warm trickle running from my ear, looking at the bright red blood on my finger.

He helped me stand. "Let's get you back to the office. The healers will take care of that."

I frowned. Surely that couldn't be right. I'd heard him say the stealers would make bear a hat. "What bear? Who are the stealers?"

Brock chuckled, shaking his head.

"No, really. What are they stealing and why a bear? Bears don't wear hats."

He wrapped an arm around my waist and helped me to the platform, where two Trolls I recognized from *Familiar, Inc.* grabbed my hands and yanked me upward. I flew into the air, sailing two feet above the ground. I landed in a crouch, glaring at the Trolls.

They shrugged, grinning. Trolls were only three to four feet high and just about as wide as they were tall, but every bit of their bulk was muscle. They sometimes forgot how strong they were.

Brock and I headed toward the public area. As we entered, my gaze slid to the closed restaurant, and I remembered. Grabbing Brock's arm, I yelled into his ear, "Deg! He's in trouble."

Brock flinched away, rubbing his ear. "You don't need to scream in *my* ear, LA. You're the one who's deaf. Not me."

I shook my head, turning away and taking off toward the restaurant. A large, black shadow swung overhead. I jolted to a halt. Energy spilled from my fingers as I prepared for battle, thinking the Wraiths were back.

Brock landed in front of me, using his enormous black wings to cut off my escape. "He's not here. Mandy has him. They're already on their way to headquarters."

I narrowed my gaze on his moving lips, trying to understand what he was telling me. Impatience made the energy in my hands sizzle. If the Demon was giving me fashion news for wildlife again, I was gonna pinch his head off.

I finally got the gist of what he was telling me and let the energy slide away. "Is Deg okay?"

Brock transformed back into his humanoid form. "The sooner we get back there, the sooner we'll know the answer to that."

Terror clawing at my lungs, I let him lead me toward the exit. I swore if Deg was hurt, somebody was going to pay. "How'd you find us?" I reached up and sent some healing magics into my ear and my hearing came back with a soft pop.

He shoved the exterior door aside. Or what was left of it. The thing was charred black with splintered edges. The frame it had been attached to was in tatters, crunching under my feet.

Apparently, Littleton's key hadn't worked for Brock...

Littleton!

"Your mother knew you'd come here first, despite the fact that she'd told you to return to the office. She sent me in case you and the Witch needed help."

"Did you find him?"

He gave me a look that said he was worried about my sanity. "The Witch? Yeah, I already told you. Mandy has him."

"Not Deg." I swallowed hard, reaching for the door handle of Brock's oversized white truck. "Littleton. Did those things...kill him?"

Brock frowned. "Just climb in. We need to report back to Queen Katherine. She's worried about you."

That was a lie. Brock or Mandy would have reported back to her immediately. "Why are you lying?"

He hit the gas and we squealed away from the curb. The back tires slipped sideways on an icy patch and then caught on a dry section of asphalt as the truck roared forward. "I'm just following orders, LA."

Orders? Why would my mother order him to lie? There was only one reason. The news was bad, and she needed my head in the game. Or, less cynically, she wanted to break it to me herself.

As a warrior, Brock was highly effective and deadly. But as a friend, the Demon wasn't the most sensitive creature. Left to his own devices, Brock would probably just blurt out that Deg was dead.

"Just give me the bad news. I need to know."

He frowned in my direction. "What bad news?"

"Don't play dumb, Demon."

He grinned. "Why, LA, our relationship has improved. There was a time when you would have just assumed I *was* dumb."

My hand tightened on my knee, pinching it as fear enveloped me. "Please, Brock."

His grin slid away. "Deg's not dead, LA."

I closed my eyes. The icy tightness in my chest eased. "Good." Then my eyes shot open again. "But is he really hurt?"

Brock expelled a sigh. "I thought the Trolls were hard to be around."

I punched his arm.

"Ouch! Dangit, LA!"

"Tell me."

"As far as I know he's *physically* unhurt."

I felt the blood leeching from my face. I remembered all too well the melting sensation and the deep depression I'd suffered from the Wraith's touch. And that had been within a few seconds. If the things had overwhelmed him and taken their time...

"No..."

"Don't assume the worst," Brock said on a frown. "The Witch is strong."

"Oh, no, no, no..." I bent over as agony twisted through my belly. I'd been unable to reach Deg through our mental communication paths. There'd been a giant void where he should have been. What if they'd destroyed his mind?

"...Littleton."

I realized with a start that Brock had been talking to me. He glanced over as I lifted my gaze in his direction. "He might never recover."

"Littleton?" I clenched my fists. "The Wraiths got him?"

Brock frowned. "I'm not sure. I found him in an abandoned car down the track. He was just lying there, looking perfectly fine. Maybe a little paler than usual. But there's nothing behind his eyes, LA." Brock shivered. "I don't have your gift for reading auras, but there was definitely something different about the Elf. Something bad."

"What do you mean, something bad?"

Brock shrugged, pulling the truck into the parking garage beneath *Familiar, Inc.* "The healers should be able to figure it out."

Thinking of Becksmart and Tollman's strange call to warn Littleton, I grabbed his arm. "Something's wrong here, Demon."

He rolled his eyes. "Ya think? That's what I've been trying to tell you."

"No, I mean beyond the obvious. Whatever it is, Tollman's freaked out and he's not talking." Brock parked the truck and turned to me. "What do you mean?"

I quickly told him what had happened at the newspaper. He listened carefully, frowning when I got to the part where Tollman ran out, clearly frazzled. "And he warned Littleton the police were coming."

"Which means he didn't believe Littleton was responsible for Becksmart's murder."

"Or he's more worried about Littleton's abilities becoming known."

Brock shook his head. "He's an Angel, LA. If he thought the Elf was killing humans, he'd stop him. He wouldn't warn him and give him a chance to escape."

An ugly thought occurred. "Except that Littleton didn't escape, did he? He was taken out by creatures who could arguably be called patrons of Heaven."

"Wraiths?" He gave me a look of pure disgust. "Try again, Wraiths are from Hell."

"Two sides of the same coin," I told him, thinking of Grandmama Celeste using them as earth-bound taxis. "The Angels have dominion over Hell, right?"

"I'm pretty sure they'd deny that emphatically."

"But you know it's true."

He shrugged. "So, what? You're saying Tollman brought the wrath of the Wraiths..." he shook his head, grinning. "... down on the Elf?"

"I think we need to consider the possibility."

He stared out the windshield at the concrete wall in front of us and then sighed. "Okay, we'll consider it. But I want to go on record saying I have trouble seeing the Angel as the vengeful type. That's more along the lines of something *my* people would do."

He wasn't wrong. Demons were volatile and held a grudge. Revenge was their favorite thing.

"Noted. Now, let's go check on my Witch. Then you and I and Mandy have a trail to follow."

Unfortunately, we weren't to be allowed to follow that

trail for a while. Politics demanded their due. My mother sent her personal assistant to meet us at the elevators. I'd never met the current PA. Ever since my mother had lost her first assistant to magical violence, she'd been going through them like water through a Troll.

I wondered if giving up her throne hadn't been a bad idea. She still had all those bossy, queenly motivations that needed an outlet.

The current unfortunate was a young man whose pale face and light blue eyes were perfectly matched to his white-blond hair and vanilla personality. However, though he seemed little more than a walking vessel of boring, he'd lasted two weeks longer than the last three assistants had. I'd begun to believe there was more to Oscar than met the eye.

I mean, there had to be, right?

He stepped forward as we opened the door from the parking garage, skinny arms clutching a magical clipboard to his narrow chest. A thick strand of white-blond hair fell into one eye and he blew on it as he hurried over to us. "LA, good. Your mother needs to see you ASAP."

I hated to make the poor guy's life more difficult, but that didn't stop me from doing exactly that. "Sorry. I need to see Deg first."

Bless Oscar's pale heart, he was one step ahead of me. He nodded while looking down at the clipboard and I followed his gaze to what looked like stick figures moving around the board. He poked at a couple of them and they scurried away, presumably bent for important destinations of his choice.

In that moment, I realized for the first time how much residual power one of my mother's assistants wielded. "We'll visit the clinic on our way to your mother's office.

You'll have two minutes to get a report from the healer. Then you'll be in a position to report his condition to the queen."

"She's no longer the queen," I felt compelled to remind him.

He nodded, stabbing a pale finger at the button on the elevator. "You'll have four point five minutes to converse privately with the queen before the rest of the council arrives."

The elevator slid open and we stepped inside. The door slipped soundlessly closed.

Oscar turned a key in the navigation panel and the back wall of the elevator disappeared, transforming to the hallway on level four, where the clinic was located.

I had to nearly run to keep up with the assistant as he hoofed it at top speed toward the glass-walled room at the end of the hall.

Turning to Brock, I arched my eyebrows in unspoken amusement. He shook his head.

Something told me Oscar would last longer than his predecessors in the assistant position. In fact, I was starting to think my mother better watch out or he'd be gunning for her job.

Oscar stopped in front of the clinic and poked at his clipboard. "Mr. Kincaide is in bed four. You'll have thirty seconds..."

We went through the door and I closed it in Oscar's face, turning the lock and giving him a wave before heading toward the healer sitting at the front desk.

She looked up as Brock and I approached, her pretty face folding into a frown. "Ms. Mapes." She stood. "Follow me."

After spending the longest two minutes of my life on

Oscar's treadmill, the healer's no-nonsense style was refreshing. She clearly had the right priorities.

The healer stopped at the door to room four and pushed it open, stepping back to allow us past. "Mandy's with him now."

I nodded. "Thanks. Can you..."

She inclined her chin. "I'll make sure Oscar doesn't make it back here."

My stomach twisting, I glanced across the room at the pale, unmoving figure on the bed.

Mandy fussed with the covers, her attention riveted on Deg and her posture tense. She looked up as we approached, and I noted the purple arcs under her caramel-colored eyes and the lines of weariness etched into the once-smooth skin of her oblong face.

She was too pale. As if she'd given Deg more of her healing energy than she should have.

I had no doubt that was the case. She and Deg had once been a couple. And if it had even been possible for me to forget that they'd once shared a special bond, I knew *she* would never forget.

A part of me suspected she still might love him. At the very least, she considered him a very close friend.

"How is he?"

Her dark brows lowered and she shook her head, the messy ponytail she'd made of her long, black hair bobbing with the movement. "I've tried everything. Something's dragging him down and I can't find it."

Her voice broke on the last word. She pressed her lips together. It was almost harder to see Mandy in that condition than it was to see Deg unmoving and as white as paper beneath the blankets. Though annoyingly over-confident, the Witch generally lived up to her high opinion of herself.

If she didn't know how to fix what had been done to Deg, I wasn't sure that anybody would.

My stomach twisted painfully at the realization. Nausea bloomed. Fear became a living thing, tearing its way through my gut. "Celeste said they were Wraiths from the Tenth circle of Hell."

Mandy nodded. "I ran up against them once, a few years ago. I watched them pull the life right out of a fellow healer. There was nothing we could do to help him."

If it was possible, she lost a little more of the color from her face. She rubbed a hand over her forehead and I noticed that it was shaking.

"They command fire and ice. Surely there's a treatment to address that."

"That's just the problem," Brock said.

When Mandy glanced at him, he lifted his midnight brows and she nodded. Apparently, they'd already discussed what he was about to share with me.

"There are magics to fix cold energy poisoning. And magics to cure hot energy overload, but they work against each other. Nothing anyone has ever done has worked against the dual nature of these Wraith's poison."

I dropped onto the edge of the bed as my knees gave out underneath me. "There has to be something..."

Mandy's gaze locked on Deg as if she were trying to will him back to health. "It's possible, with time, that Deg could recover from the poison if that were all he was fighting."

"What do you mean?" I asked her softly. I had trouble forming the question because I was afraid I already knew the answer.

And I didn't like it.

"They infused him with their own unique poison. And once his body was tainted, they feasted on his mind." Her lips quivered and when she looked up at me, a single tear trickled down her colorless cheek.

It hit me like a blow to the chest. I couldn't breathe. "That's not possible," I gasped out. Though I knew it was true. I'd experienced the beginnings of his fate myself. If not for Celeste's interference, I'd have been in the same boat as Deg.

I blinked, surging off the bed. "Celeste!"

Mandy frowned. "She's gone, LA. She can't help."

"She's only gone from this plane, Mandy. You of all people should understand that. She saved me from those things. She lives in their world. Maybe she knows of some way to help."

I braced for the Witch's censure, knowing that her ego was wrapped up in healing my partner.

But she looked me in the eye and said three words that sent fear and dread down my spine like acid-drenched claws.

"Okay. Try it."

That was the moment I knew, without a doubt, that I was going to lose Deg.

NINE

Oscar was frantically punching his clipboard when Brock and I emerged from the clinic. He looked up and glared at me, blowing hair out of his eyes with violent force. "You've put the entire schedule behind with your antics."

I walked right up to him and stabbed him in his scrawny chest with a finger. "I don't work for you. You back off, now!"

Oscar slammed his lips closed, but none of the fire left his pale blue eyes as he stepped backward, clipboard clutched against his chest, and motioned for me to pass on by.

I knew I'd have to apologize to him later. After all, he was just doing his job. But I was in crisis, and I didn't have time for his pencil pushing tactics at the moment.

I hurried down the hall and into the waiting elevator with Brock on my heels. The Demon was uncharacteristically quiet. When I glanced his way, I saw the worry reflected in his dark gaze.

Brock had apparently come to the same conclusion about Deg as I had. "We're going to fix this," I all but growled out. He nodded, but I didn't get the sense that he believed me.

When the door opened on level twenty, I looked up at him. "Talk to all the magic houses. Find somebody who's dealt with this before. I don't care if we need to make a trip to Axismundi, we're going to heal him."

Brock's gaze sharpened and he inclined his chin, some of the tension leaching from his handsome face. "I won't overlook any option, LA. I promise."

Nodding my thanks, I stalked toward my mother's rooms at the end of the hall. I marched inside without announcing myself and found her standing before the floor to ceiling windows that overlooked *Illusion City*.

She turned slowly and looked at me with an expression that gave none of her feelings away. It was her Queen Katherine face. She'd gotten very good at hiding her feelings over the years. "How is he?"

I appreciated her asking the question before she began demanding my time and attention. The truth was, she wasn't going to get any of my attention for council matters until I'd figured out how to help my Witch. "Not good. I need to speak to Celeste."

Two lines appeared in her smooth brow. "LeeAnn..."

I held up a hand. "She knows about these things. She might know how we can fight this poison they injected into Deg."

Mother considered my suggestion and then nodded. "We can call her back for a short visit. I'll need to get special dispensation from the *Elysian Fields*."

"Do it!"

Her brow furrowed, and I lifted a hand in apology. "Please?"

She nodded. "Consider it done. What else can I do?"

"I need every healer you have working on this. Mandy's in charge. But we need to get creative and fast. Or we're going to lose him."

A small smile played about my mother's lips. I was pretty sure I knew what she was smiling about, but I didn't have time to think about it. "And we might need to go through the portal."

The portal to *Underworld* or *Axismundi* was normally only used once or twice a year for council business. It was dangerous. Every time we breached it, we risked bringing something deadly back with us. I watched her expression tighten against the idea, but to my shock, she nodded. "If it's absolutely necessary."

"Good." I started to pace the room.

Mother watched me pace for a moment and then said, "Littleton has shown some small improvement."

I stopped and looked at her, shocked. "Really?"

"Yes. The healers are still not optimistic, but any improvement at all is pretty phenomenal."

My mind raced. "Maybe he's got some kind of natural immunity. We could use that."

"LA!"

I realized how cold I sounded. I'd probably feel bad about it later. But in that moment, all I could think about was saving Deg. "It's a practical solution, Mother. We can't affect Littleton's recovery. Everyone keeps telling me that. But if something we learn from him can help Deg..."

I let the words trail away, suddenly ashamed. "I'm a horrible person."

I heard the gentle swish of her fitted silk suit as she walked toward me. The soft sweetness of her perfume assailed me as she wrapped me in a hug. "We'll do everything we can to help him, peaches."

"I know." I sighed. "I'm having trouble breathing."

She held me a moment longer and then stepped away, tipping my chin up with a cool fingertip. "Talk to Trudy. She might have some ideas. She lived in *Axismundi* for a long time."

I nodded. Mother was right. My aunt just might know something that could help. "Is she in her rooms?"

"I believe she is."

I started for the door, stopping with my hand on the knob and turning back. "About the council..."

"I'll deal with that. We've already put measures into place to stop the human news from exposing us. I'm sad to say Littleton's current condition has helped to solve that particular problem. You focus on Deg. Hopefully, whatever you find will help Littleton too. Don't worry about the rest."

I nodded again, tears burning my eyes at my mother's understanding and kindness. Then I let myself out of her rooms and headed toward the elevator. The more I thought about my mother's suggestion about talking to my aunt, the more excited I became.

Trudy had dealt with *Underworld* magics. She'd developed some unique skills of her own while there. She actually might be able to help.

I clung to that thought. Because, if I didn't have something to hope for. I was afraid I'd succumb to the despair I'd tasted in my short interaction with those horrible Wraiths.

TRUDY WAS STANDING in her doorway when I exited the elevator. She'd been under careful watch during the weeks since she'd returned to the human plane from *Underworld*. But she'd recently been sprung from her controlled environment and given an apartment one floor beneath my mother's and Celeste's. Since my grandmama's death, Mother had tried to get her sister to move upstairs. But Trudy had resisted. She'd insisted that she preferred the smaller but still very comfortable rooms on a floor she inhabited all by herself. Two other apartments were empty on the floor, and I knew my mother hoped one day that I'd move into one of them. But I enjoyed my privacy too much.

And no way did I want to live that close to my mother.

Trudy reached for my hands as I approached. "Your mother called me. I'm so sorry about your Witch."

I nodded, clasping her hands.

She grimaced. "Your fingers are like ice." She wrapped them in her own hands and a soft, pink glow emerged, sending delicious warmth through my skin. "There, that's better."

She avoided my gaze as she dropped my hands. I realized she was dreading our coming conversation and I couldn't help wondering why.

"Did Mother tell you what I needed to talk to you about?"

Instead of answering, she turned back into her apartment, motioning for me to join her. I closed the door and stood there, my nerves jumping.

"Sit, LeeAnn. I'll get you some tea."

"I don't want..."

She motioned toward the couch. "It will calm you so you can think more clearly."

I had to agree that was a good idea. "Okay. Thanks." I sat but soon realized it was impossible to stay still, so I got back up and paced around the room.

I stopped in front of a long cabinet that held a dozen framed family pictures. I reached out and touched a photo from when I was about eight years old. I stood between Mother and Trudy in front of a brightly colored carousel. I remembered that carousel and the fair that came every summer to *Illusion City*. My finger caressed the rolled, silver frame and a wistful mood slid over me. What I wouldn't give to have even one-tenth of the simplicity of those days back again.

"Here."

I took a steaming cup of tea from Trudy. "Thank you, Auntie." I lifted the cup and sniffed it, glancing up. "Passion Flower?"

She nodded. "And skullcap, which will purge some of the tension in your muscles."

I sipped, wincing at the bitterness.

"That's the skullcap," Trudy said, watching me until I'd taken several sips. The heat of the tea eased through me, making me feel almost instantly better. "This is great."

She nodded and motioned toward the couch again. "Can you sit now?" She smiled to take the sting from the rebuke. I was probably making her nervous with all my pacing.

"I'll try."

Once we were both seated on the couch, she stared at her hands, clasped in her lap, for a moment before she spoke. "I bumped up against Wraiths from all states of Hell when I was in *Axismundi*. Horrible creatures."

She wouldn't get any argument from me on that. "Do you know how to counteract their poison?"

She unclasped her hands, her long fingers plucking at her slacks as she seemed to be considering my question. Finally, she looked up, her gaze locking onto mine. She opened her mouth to respond and hesitated, finally shaking her head. "No."

I could tell by the way she was acting that wasn't the truth. "Trudy, whatever it is, I want to try it. Deg will die if we don't do something."

"It's not possible."

"Then we'll need to make it possible. Just tell me."

She stood up and walked over to the cabinet with all the pictures. Her posture was rigid, and she seemed to be fighting with herself about whether to tell me what I wanted to know.

I settled my teacup onto the table and went to stand beside her. Without a word, I slipped my arm around her waist and rested my head on her shoulder. Despite my best efforts, tears slipped from my eyes. "Please, Auntie."

She took a shuddering breath and rested her head on mine. "I promised your grandmother I'd keep you safe."

"Celeste knew that wasn't possible," I said on a watery laugh. "She was just tweaking you."

Trudy laughed too, and I heard her own tears in the sound. "I wouldn't put that past her."

I pointed to the carnival picture. "I remember that day. You bought me caramel corn and cotton candy and Mother yelled at you for sugaring me up."

She sniffed, but when I looked up she was smiling. "It was the best day, wasn't it?"

"The very best. I was a very lucky little girl to have so many people who loved me. I didn't fully appreciate it then, but I do now. When I was eight, I needed you to protect me. Now, I need you to recognize that I'm an adult and treat me as such. You can't protect me, Auntie, because I won't let you. I'm capable of protecting myself."

She stared at the picture a moment longer and then sighed. "The old magic eater was definitely tweaking me."

I laughed again.

"Okay. Go pack a bag. And bring lots of potions. It's not going to be an easy trip. We can probably use the Demon too."

"I'll tell him," I said, heading for the door.

"Have you spoken to the Angel?"

I turned back. "Tollman? Not since he ran out on us at the newspaper. Why do you ask?"

She frowned. "The Tenth Wraiths are not subject to call. Not like the lesser Wraiths. They can't be ridden like Celeste rides hers and they can't be summoned."

"Are you telling me the Wraiths acted alone?" I didn't like the sound of that. If Wraiths had decided to attack the human realm we were going to have a huge mess on our hands.

It would bring new meaning to the term, all hell breaking loose.

"That's unlikely. Wraiths are more comfortable in their own realm. They aren't generally adventurous and most likely wouldn't choose to step outside their comfort zone."

"Then what?"

I didn't like the look in her eyes. It was beyond worry, dabbling in the realm of terrified.

"They can be compelled through a Celestial mandate."

My pulse spiked, blowing any helpful effects of Trudy's tea right out of my system. "Angelic?"

She shrugged. "That seems the most likely source, yes."

No wonder Tollman had run from the room. Then I had a thought that gave me hope. "Can Tollman reverse the effects of the poison?"

"No. The Wraiths can be compelled, but their methods are their own. And the results of those methods are almost always irreversible."

Hope crashed. "But you know of something we can try, right?"

"I know of something that *might* work. There are no guarantees, LeeAnn. I need you to understand that before we leave."

"It will work," I said with a conviction I didn't feel.

"Child..."

I held up a hand. "It will work, Auntie. Because it has to."

TEN

Axismundi, or Underworld as human legend referred to it, served as a gateway to all other dimensions. There were twelve distinct dimensions or realms, and *Axismundi* fed into them all.

We were headed toward the Hades Realm, and to get there, we had to first travel to *Axismundi.* Getting there took several hours through a long portal built inside a mountain. Once we arrived, the journey across *Axismundi* was fraught with the usual perils, creature and environmentally based. Aside from the unending blackness and the thick miasma of sulfur in the air, the bleakness of the landscape was its own kind of torture, making our already dour moods even more bitter.

And of course there was the usual boiling black mire that moved and shifted around us, which made sticking to the narrow path through its center nearly impossible. Unfortunately, falling from the path was a fatal mistake.

The whole ugly package had shaken us as we traveled across the unwelcoming place. An air of dread had settled over our party like an itchy blanket. Even Brock, who in some ways was right at home in the Demon-saturated land, was unusually quiet and morose.

Trudy was quiet too, though she seemed unaffected otherwise, and the five Trolls we'd brought with us wore dour expressions and had their heads continually on a swivel, their muscular forms taut with wariness.

I couldn't help wondering, watching him shift his shoulders for about the hundredth time, if he wasn't wishing he could break out his demonic form and fly away from it all.

I certainly wished I could.

I scrubbed the back of my hand over my forehead, which was wet with sweat from the super-tropical temps and the total lack of any kind of breeze. "How much longer?" I asked my aunt.

Trudy skimmed her gaze to me. I marveled at the calm I saw there. I felt like a sweaty, filthy slug next to her. It wasn't only the tranquil expression and the fact that she didn't appear to have sweated a single drop since leaving the passageway and stepping foot into the forbidding place. It was the perfect red-gold hair, falling in glossy waves over a pristine white cotton shirt tucked into slim, multi-pocketed cargo pants in a still-spotless light khaki color.

My own hair was a dusty, tangled mass that stuck to my face and neck and dripped with sweat. My tee-shirt was saturated, my jeans filthy and torn. In short, I was literally a hot mess.

Trudy took one look at me and lifted her arm, calling a halt to our small procession. "We'll rest for a while here."

I dropped to a tree stump with a groan, shoving curly red hair off my face and reaching to pull the hair band from its messy length so I could tighten it up again. "My feet are killing me."

Trudy stood over me, her lips twitching with humor.

"I'm thinking back to that wonderful and moving speech you gave me about how you're so self-sufficient and can take care of yourself."

"Shut up, Auntie."

She chuckled and the sound was swallowed up in the thick air as if it had never existed.

"Do you have any water? I drank all of mine about ten miles back."

She lifted a red-gold brow. "LeeAnn. You'll die without water. I told you to bring enough for several days."

"I know, but I thought you were just exaggerating. This trip can't possibly take that long."

"Can't it?" she asked me sardonically.

I held out my hand. "Besides, I knew you'd bring extra."

She expelled a sigh and motioned to one of the Trolls up the path a distance. He ambled back to us, his broad form made even wider by the enormous packs he wore on each shoulder and strapped over his hips. He wasn't even sweating or breathing hard.

Trolls were truly the pack animal of the magic world.

"Deergart, the princess needs water."

I glared at my aunt. She didn't mean princess as in the daughter of the queen. Especially since my mother no longer claimed that title. She was making an unkind remark about my heartiness. "Har- de-har, Auntie."

Deergart's chest rumbled and I realized that was him laughing. He reached a short-fingered hand into the pack around his waist and pulled out a bottle of water, handing it to me. The fingers wrapped around the bottle were wide and blunt, each digit the width of two of mine. The nails were tidy and carefully clipped. Deergart didn't appear to be suffering under the filth and heat either. Apparently, it was just me.

"Thanks, Deer."

He grinned, the bumpy skin of his greenish face folding in wide wrinkles on either side of the smile. His teeth were large and squared off like the rest of him, shaped like Chiclets, straight and white. "Do you need a bar?" Deergart asked me in a voice that sounded like rocks plunging down a mountainside.

"Sure."

He reached into a deep pocket on the inside of the pack over his left shoulder and pulled out a protein bar. They'd been specially developed at *Familiar, Inc.* to support the unique protein needs of a magic user. We also sold them to humans for ridiculously high prices. They were healthy and kept non-magic-users, who didn't use nearly as much energy as we did, satisfied for hours.

Plus we magicked them to taste like pure decadence.

Brock came over and took a bar too. He ate his in three bites, then looked at Trudy as Deergart handed him some water.

See, I wasn't the only one who'd run out of water. I didn't hear anybody calling Brock princess.

I snorted at the thought and Deergart winked as if he was in on the joke. He might have been. Some Trolls were blessed with the inner sight. They could see other people's random thoughts in pictures in their minds, which was way weird, and was the reason I'd occasionally see one of them break into tears or laughter for no apparent reason.

I'd have to keep an eye on Deer and avoid having any private or embarrassing thoughts around him.

"I'm going to go up and scout ahead," Brock told Trudy.

She shook her head. "We need to stick together."

He scowled. "I won't be gone long. You know it's better if I scope out the trail before we walk it."

Trudy seemed to be considering his suggestion.

I could see the tension in Brock's tall form, and I knew he needed to go. "Let him, Auntie. Brock knows this area. He can see trouble we won't be able to see." Sometimes *Axismundis* were dangerously good at hiding. "We also have to worry about the remnants of Reginald's army. He's still got loyalists who'd love to get hold of you and me."

Reginald was the wizard who'd kept Trudy captive when she'd lived in *Axismundi*. He'd been imprisoned for his crimes, but he still had loyal followers across the realm.

She finally nodded. "Okay, but only go out a couple of miles. We're going to stop for the night soon anyway."

Brock nodded, swallowed half of his water in one gulp, and then gave me a look filled with gratitude before taking a running leap and exploding into his demonic form.

Trudy watched, her expression taut, as Brock's thirty-foot expanse of bat-like wings undulated gracefully on the steamy air.

"He'll be fine," I told her. "He needs to let off a little steam."

"I know." She gave me a small smile. "We should reach the barrier for the Tenth in a few hours. As soon as we cross we'll be in constant danger. We need to rest up tonight."

I chewed my bar, my gaze still on the darkened sky above. The heat of the place pulsed against my skin as I sat there. Even my sweat couldn't cool me because there was no breeze to make it work. I couldn't imagine how hot it was going to be when we reached the Tenth circle.

Trudy dropped down next to me, a soft groan escaping her lips. It was the first sign she'd given of being tired.

I glanced her way. "What's it like?"

"Hmm?" She nibbled a protein bar, her expression calm.

"The Tenth. What is it like? Is it really a circle?"

She swallowed, shaking her head. "That's a myth. The circles are actually states, broken up millennia ago for the purposes of controlling the inhabitants."

"Controlling? How?"

She took another small bite and then shoved the bar back into its wrapper and slipped it into the pack she'd set alongside the stump. "Well, aside from there being ten territories instead of nine, there is some truth to the division of souls into the ten states. The worse a soul's crimes, the higher the number of the state they're placed into."

"The Tenth is used as a threat, to keep in check those who might consider being even more evil?"

"Yes."

Which meant the Wraiths in the Tenth truly were the worst of the worst. "These Wraiths we're about to go up against. They're corrupted souls?"

She frowned slightly, unscrewing the lid from her water bottle. "In the most basic sense, yes. But it's actually more complicated than that. When they entered Hades, the Wraiths might have been First State candidates. But something twisted inside them." She looked around, grimacing. "This place will do it to even the best among us."

"They fell further from grace?"

"There is no grace in the states, LeeAnn. But there are levels of debauchery and monstrosity. The same influences that turn people to the wrong side when they're alive blacken their souls once they enter a state."

"Hades changes them...their souls...irretrievably?" I thought I was beginning to understand. "Does everyone eventually succumb?"

"Most do. But those who manage to keep to the light for

a decade in the First State are sometimes risen to the Angelic Choir."

When I looked shocked, she shook her head. "Think about it, child. What they did to be sent here in the first place aside, those people hold onto their last shred of goodness under near impossible odds. They're exactly the type of souls who belong with the Angels. They understand human temptation like no others. They've earned their spots in the Choir."

I could definitely see that. "They go to Heaven?"

"No. Some are sent to watch over the Human Realm, though they are few and under strict governance to keep them from affecting the course of the future in that realm."

I wondered if Tollman had been one of those. It would certainly explain his fashion sense. "And the rest?"

"They're called Watchers. They patrol the other states, judging the behavior of others and moving them from state to state as required."

My eyes widened. "They're still stuck here? That's horrible."

Trudy shrugged. "Maybe. But they have benefits the others don't. They don't feel the heat. They're not affected by the despair that throbs through the atmosphere in every state. They live with comforts and pleasures even some in the Human Realm might envy."

I thought about what she told me for a long moment. I'd had no idea Hades was so complex. My mind returned to the Tenth. "You said it was more than corrupted souls that made the Tenth Wraiths. What else?"

"It is complete corruption, you're right about that. But it's more. They become the embodiment of what is evil and wrong. They shrivel up into little more than ugliness and despair. Every trial they ever suffered, every pain they ever inflicted is played back to them a thousand times a day. They lose the will to survive but have no choice. Their very withering—a drying out process not unlike curing leather—has turned them nearly indestructible. Part of their punishment is that they are forced to constantly relive their sins, only experience them as their victims did, without a way to escape the pain. It's a horrible existence."

"And the fiery pits?"

"That's where they spend the first hundred years of their existence in the Tenth. It winnows them down to nothing but hate and despair."

"You said almost nothing can kill them. How are we supposed to fight them off long enough to find what we're looking for?"

Two lines appeared between her red-gold brows. "That's a good question."

"We could use the flowers, right?" We'd come to Underworld to find a rare flower that was deadly to Wraiths. It was located only in the Tenth and was heavily protected. Getting one was going to be very difficult. Finding one before the Wraiths found us would be nearly impossible.

She nodded. "If we're lucky enough to find one in time, yes. While in the Tenth, they emit a gas that gives the Wraiths a kind of death. Though it's worse than what they called living."

"But if they're meant to suffer through eternity for their crimes..."

"Why create the flower?" Her smile was lacking in humor. "A back door. Something that is truly impervious to death would be a terrible risk. As we've seen, they can cause great damage if they escape to the other realms."

"Do they escape very often?"

She turned to me, fixing me with a cold, terrifying gaze. "It's never happened before."

"Then how...?"

"I don't know. Something's afoot. And we need to get to the bottom of it before all hell literally breaks loose. Mother is looking into it."

"Celeste? You spoke to her?" I'd tried to contact Grandmama again before we left, but she wasn't responding. She'd never ignored me before. I'd been fretting about it the entire trip.

"Yes. She agrees with me that the whole humans-learning-about-magic debacle was meant to distract us. We just don't know how the Wraiths were able to enter the Human Realm. From everything we've read, it should be impossible. Unless..."

"Unless, what?"

The sound of wings throbbing on the air brought our heads up. Brock was so dark he melted into the inky sky, unseen, until he dropped low enough to be caught in the faint glow the ground beneath us continually gave off in *Axismundi*.

As soon as we saw him, we knew he was bringing trouble back with him. He was flying fast and furious, and even from a distance, I had no trouble making out the look of pure terror on his handsome face.

ELEVEN

"Trudy," I said, jumping to my feet.

Her gaze flew skyward, following mine, and then skimmed across the inky layers of night above and behind Brock. She grabbed for her pack. "Dark Fairies." Trudy yanked a vial of something from her bag and slid her gaze my way. "This would be a good time to pull out some of the potions I told you to bring."

I was way ahead of her, having already pulled a jar from my pack. I was just waiting for Brock to get closer.

The first Fairy hit the ground and skidded toward us, its knife-like teeth bared in a snarl as it slashed toward Deergart with a blade that flashed pale green light across the night.

The Troll threw himself to the side and rolled, no small feat given the fact that he was laden with packs, and came up with a short, wide blade made of Troll-iron.

I'd handled one of the swords once and had barely been able to lift it off the ground with two hands.

Deergart swung it easily, turning the Fairy's tiny sword into Fairy dust with one accurate strike. He growled something in the guttural language favored by his race, and the other pack-bearers dropped their packs to take up their own swords.

Brock growled my name and my gaze shot toward the boiling mass above my head.

He was flying backward, his big form covered in small, black bodies that nipped and slashed at him with their magic blades.

The light show of their attack was beautiful. If only I didn't know that every third slice found its mark.

I could see the effectiveness of their attack in Brock's too-quick descent. He hit the ground too fast and fell backward, skidding several feet before finding his feet again.

Trudy had pulled a long knife from her pack and was using it very effectively against the rabid little Fairies.

I opened the jar in my hand and set it down on the ground, my fingers dancing on the air as I crafted the spell that would guide its use. The potion had been designed to exterminate anything which didn't have the mark of the human realm in its aura. I probably shouldn't have brought it. The outcome was too unpredictable and therefore dangerous. If the magic wasn't precise enough, I could inadvertently kill the Trolls or even my demonic friend. But there were just too many of the Fairies for us to win the battle without something pretty drastic.

I skimmed the waiting Fairies above us another look. I didn't like that they weren't attacking. I needed them closer for the spell to work.

The Hades version of Fairies were small, with black wings that flashed color like their blades as they throbbed against the sky. Where Brock's thirty-foot wide expanse of wing was strong and deadly, the Fairies' wings were delicate and ineffectual in battle, except for the agility they afforded them. An agility Brock could never match. Their small bodies danced lightly on the air, attacking and then leaping easily away before a counterstrike could find them.

They attacked with teeth, blade, and claw.

I'd never seen the Dark Fairies of Hades before, but I'd heard enough about them to know the danger with them was in the accumulation of damage. A determined Fairy could create a hundred wounds in minutes, weakening their opponents through the sheer number of strikes.

Individually they were easy to kill. Their real strength was in their vast numbers, as illustrated by what looked like hundreds of the nasty things waiting in the sky above our heads.

Why they hadn't all attacked us yet was a mystery I needed to solve if we were going to survive the attack.

I finished my spell and tied it off, waiting with my fingers poised above the jar. All it would take would be a jolt of energy to ignite the spell. But the spell was a one-time deal. I couldn't release it until the bulk of the attacking Fairies moved close.

Pain seared across my shoulders, a slice that stung at first and then flared into agony as I straightened and turned.

Two of the little devils charged me, slashing viciously at my face and arms. I shot an arrow of energy into the first one, sending it flying backward to smack against a tree. The Fairy bounced off and came right back at me, ducking low to slash my thighs as its friend continued to slice the flesh of my upper body.

I panicked, sending energy flying wildly around me. A yelp and a growl told me that one of my shots had found the wrong mark.

"Hold your magic, Familiar!" Deergart growled in my direction.

"Sorry!" I yelled as I ducked to avoid another attack from the Fairies. Power arrows weren't going to cut it. I needed some other way to kill the nasty bugs.

Then I had an idea. It was a bit risky, but drastic times called for drastic measures.

I grabbed my pack and barely had time to lift it off the ground before they were on me again. In a moment of sheer desperation, I swung the pack at them, letting my rage escape in a primal scream. The pack did its work, sending them flying right into Brock's big, demonic hands. He snatched them right out of the air and ripped them in half, green blood flying everywhere.

Grimacing as some of the greasy green stuff landed on me, I shoved my hand into my pack and pulled out a stunning spell. It would halt anything it encountered immediately. The trick would be to send it high enough to only grab the Fairies.

I glanced at Brock, who roared in rage as he plucked two more of the nasty bugs off his back and crushed them, his dagger-like teeth exposed on a snarl. "Get ready to hit the ground, I told him. Cover your face."

He didn't respond. He was too busy trying to flick Fairies off his wings.

I glanced at Deergart and he nodded as he dispatched another Fairy, turning it into sparks on the air with his blade.

I needed one of those blades. Maybe in a kitchen knife size so I could lift it.

I glanced around, looking for my aunt. "Trudy!"

I didn't see her at first, and fear made my chest tighten. I spun in a circle, searching the darkness. I finally found her several yards away, seemingly holding her own with several of the Fairies, who danced light on the air around her head, getting in as many slicing blows as they could.

Trudy was covered in blood, her face a mass of cuts and her arms even more torn up, as I had no doubt she used them to protect herself from the attacks.

I heard the telltale buzz of wings and ducked as two more Fairies did a drive-by of my head. "Trudy, get ready to duck!"

She bent low and swung sideways, then lifted her blade and slashed it across the middle of the Fairy nearest her. She spared me a quick look and a nod.

I turned the lid on the potion jar and yelled, "Now!" sending energy into the bubbling gray potion and throwing the jar as hard as I could into the air.

I swung away, my fingers dancing on a spell that would immobilize the Fairies long enough for me to end them.

The potion ignited in a flash of white light as I hit the ground. I heard the grunts of the others as they threw themselves to the rocky ground and then the soft, *plop, plop, plop* of the stunned Fairies as they fell.

Several of them landed on me, and I suffered a painful stab in the back of the arm as one of their blades found my flesh when it fell.

I climbed to my feet, groaning. Everything hurt. I looked around and saw Brock, Trudy, and the Trolls pushing off the ground.

Well, all but one Troll.

Deergart wobbled on his feet, his wide face an unmoving mask as he oh-so-slowly toppled forward, crunching a pile of stunned Fairies beneath his heavy body.

He was going to be really ticked when he came to.

"Incoming!" Brock yelled.

I heard the roar in the sky that told me the Fairies who'd

been waiting above us were on the move. My gaze shot to the jar of magic I'd prepped to take them down. I realized I would never reach it in time. I took off running just as the first wave of Fairies hit, teeth bared and swords flaring against the darkness.

I managed to send a power arrow into two of them as they dived toward me, but a third sunk its teeth into my shoulder and shook its head like a dog.

I screamed, spinning as I tried to dislodge the nasty bug.

Blood ran in warm rivulets down my arm, and my vision turned gray from the pain.

The Fairy was too close for me to hit it with an energy jolt. In sheer desperation, I slammed my shoulder into a tree, shrieking in agony as the impact made the thing's teeth rip deeper into me. But the Fairy released me upon impact. I wrapped my fingers around its throat and threw it as hard as I could against the tree, hitting it with magic as it slid to the ground.

There was a low-level hum in the air. It vibrated in my chest and made my pulse spike with nerves. At first, I thought it was from the Fairies' wings, but the cadence wasn't right. The sound grew as I stumbled toward my potion, digging into my nerves like razor-sharp blades.

The Fairies' mouths were open and they were singing the vibrations on the air like a song.

The sound rattled me, made me so jumpy the slightest movement had me leaping sideways, shooting energy haphazardly around the space.

With a roar of half anger and half irrational fear, I slashed my way to the potion and dropped down to my knees beside it.

I pulled energy into my fingertips and prepared to send it into the potion, igniting the killing magic inside.

But something slammed into me, sending me to the ground. I was flattened under an object that felt like a boulder and smelled like a field of freshly-mown grass.

One of Deergart's Trolls had apparently succumbed to the vibrations.

Warm blood ran down my cheek, and I was pretty sure it wasn't mine. Gasping for breath, I shoved at the unconscious Troll, but he wasn't moving.

With a growing sense of terror, I looked up to find several Fairies hovering above me, their terrifying teeth gleaming red in the light of their deadly swords.

They eyed my throat, no doubt seeing my death in their minds.

And I couldn't move.

I couldn't even slow them down.

If I didn't figure something out really fast, I was going to die.

I tugged on my trapped hands, thinking if I could get one free, I could send energy into the jar that waited several feet away.

It was a longshot. If I didn't hit the potion just right it would misfire, wasting what was possibly our only shot at escaping the Fairies.

I managed to move one hand a few inches, but not enough to reach around the fallen Troll. I tried shifting my body and my cheek bumped up against something sharp, creating a painful burning that I suspected was a new slice across my skin.

The buzzing noise from the things above me increased, and their wings cleaved the air more quickly. They were about to attack.

I'd run out of time.

I stretched my body as much as I could and turned my

head, seeing the Troll's sword perched against my chest, the hilt stuck in the rocky soil. The Troll must have dropped it as it fell. It had come within inches of slicing off my head.

But it hadn't. And I had an idea. I let the energy drain from my hands and dug into my stash of power words, finding the ones I needed just as the Fairies attacked.

TWELVE

"*Resurgemus percutiens*," I screamed as the deadly bugs plunged downward. The energy from the words spun once and then shot into the sword, ripping it from the ground. It rose straight up with a hiss of power and slashed sideways, turning two of the Fairies into dust. The sword completed its work handily, finishing off five more hovering bugs before a big hand snatched it from the air.

Brock's face appeared above the Troll. "Hey," he said with a smile. His teeth shone white in the demonic blackness of his handsome face.

"Hey, yourself. Do you think you can get this oaf off me before I'm completely crushed?"

With a quick glance above his head, he lifted an arm and slashed the air, exploding several more Fairies. "Sure." He eyed the short, unattractive blade. "I need one of these."

I snickered. Between the two of us, we managed to roll the Troll off onto the dust-covered ground. Brock gave me a hand up, using the sword to remove several more flying nemeses as he did. "These things are getting on my nerves," he grumbled.

I nodded. "Mine too. How about we get rid of them?"

"Sounds like a plan," he responded, before spinning away and putting the sword he'd just acquired to good use.

I hurried over to my waiting potion and pulled energy into my hands, glancing quickly around to take stock of my friends before igniting the swirling blue liquid inside the jar. "Bug control!" I yelled before sending a healthy dose of energy into the roiling potion.

The liquid inside the jar retracted beneath the jolt and hardened into a thick crust on the bottom. The blue turned to black and the dried-up husk of the magic chipped away, floating toward the top of the jar.

I frowned down at it, wondering if I'd made a dud.

I certainly hoped not. My friends were still screaming in pain all around me from the nasty Fairies.

"Hurry up, LA," Brock yelled at me. "I'm having trouble keeping them away from you."

"I don't know what..." A puff of dust flew from the jar, hitting me right in the face.

I jerked backward just in time to keep from taking a blast of concentrated magic right in the face. The energy blew straight up from the jar, a putrid yellow color that was filled with small particles which swirled through the glow. It spread in a flash and illuminated the flying Fairies, turning their small, mean eyes red.

The bugs stopped attacking and blinked at the light, their confusion clear. I had a second moment of uncertainty, worrying that the potion had delivered shock and awe but not much else. Then the first fairy stiffened, its eyes rolling back into its head, and dropped like a rock to the ground. All around it, more and more Fairies succumbed, until the ground was littered with the nasty things.

Filled with a sense of relief, I dragged an arm over my

face. It came away dark with soot from the potion. "Is everybody okay?"

There was a beat of silence, and my gaze swung around the battlefield in a moment of panic. "Hello?"

What if I'd killed them all?

Trudy and Brock stood in front of me, looks of perplexity on their faces. One by one, the Trolls sauntered up, heavy swords drooping as they peered at me, wide-eyed.

Deergart ambled over, unsteady on his feet from the first blast of my errant magic. He narrowed his gaze, cocked his head, and then scrubbed a square hand over his wide chin. "Am I magic-drunk, or is she supposed to be that color?"

His words seemed to break the spell everyone was under. Laughter burst around me. And I huffed out a sigh. I was torn between begging for a mirror and living in denial.

I finally shrugged. I've heard de-Nile is beautiful in the Spring.

———

"NO, really, you should look in the mirror," Brock said again, his laughter filled with delight.

I was just as pleased as punch I could entertain him by looking like a clown. "I don't want to see it."

"But it's such a nice mix of colors," he choked out, before succumbing to another round of helpless laughter.

The Trolls plodding along behind us joined in too, their laughter resembling a landslide of rocks pinging against a field of cymbals. Slightly musical but annoying just the same. "I'm so happy you're all enjoying my misfortune," I bit out.

Trudy looked at me, her lips twitching. "If it's any consolation, I think some of the colors are fading."

I grimaced. "Great, then I'll have a striped face instead of one that looks like a rainbow."

Brock went off again like a jovial rocket.

I shook my head. "Juvenile."

"I can try to remove it," Trudy said, narrowing her gaze on my face. "It might not all come off since it's your spell, but I can maybe dull the colors a little." Her lips twitched again. "The purple in particular is really bright. It might take several tries to get it all."

Hilarity filled the air behind me.

I sighed. "It's okay. As soon as we stop I'll do a reversal spell."

"You really shouldn't have put your face right down in the potion jar, child."

It almost killed me, but I held my tongue. We walked another half mile, and I tried not to think about how tired I was. I'd used a lot of magic fighting off the Fairies. I needed food and rest to restore my energy. Problem was, I still had magic to do when we stopped, and I was so tired I didn't even feel like eating.

Trudy rubbed the hem of her shirt over her face. The thin fabric came away red with blood. "I wish you'd let me heal you, Auntie.

"There'll be time for that later, after we're safely home. You need to conserve your strength. We'll need it tomorrow."

We trudged on in silence for a while. Then, in an effort to keep from thinking about my aching feet, I decided to find out exactly what we were going into the Tenth in search of.

"Auntie?"

"Mm-hm." Her voice was soft, her gaze far away.

"Tell me about this flower we're going to collect."

"Genus Lilium. It's white, with long, spiky leaves and blood-red stamen that produce poison instead of pollen. In this realm, lilies are highly magical. In fact, a very small amount of the magic we're seeking still remains in the earth-grown lily. That's why humans are so fond of them for funerals. Though I'm sure they don't understand the desire to include them in the practice of burying their dead."

I thought about that for a minute. "I guess there's not enough of the magic to help Deg and Littleton?"

"No. We'd need a whole city full of earth lilies to help even the smallest amount. These flowers are called *dulcemori*."

I frowned. "Sweet death? What a strange name for a flower that makes Wraiths into the living dead."

She nodded. "There are only a few of them in the Tenth, and they grow slowly. They're one of only a handful of things that can grow in that horrible climate. And the only pleasant thing I know of there. The Wraiths guard them with savage dedication."

"But why? If the flowers can be used to give them a forever death which is worse than what they're living in the Tenth, why wouldn't they just destroy them?"

She glanced my way, looking thoughtful. "Are you familiar with the State Prophecies?"

I shook my head.

"Each of the ten states has a prophecy. It's written in the tenth prophecy that, if a Wraith tries to destroy a single *dulcemori* petal, a dozen more will appear and their danger multiplies twelve-fold."

"A pretty good deterrent," I said, smiling.

"Yes," she agreed.

An hour later, when I could barely drag myself another foot and I thought I'd lose my mind from the heat and the sticky sweat covering my entire body, Trudy's head came up and she stopped, looking around. "We're here."

I didn't even care where we were. I was just glad to stop walking. I started to lower my butt to a large rock, and my legs gave out halfway. I hit the smooth surface hard and almost bounced off again.

Brock and Deergart came up on either side of Trudy. The three of them stood staring at something ahead of us on the path.

Nosiness finally overcame weariness, and I turned my head to look too. I blinked, not sure at first what I was seeing.

Then I saw them. They'd blended into the night at first, and it took me a moment to pull their shapes from the surrounding darkness

Several shadowy creatures with elongated limbs and glowing orange eyes stood facing us, hauntingly still.

Wraiths!

"How'd they know?" Brock asked Trudy in a low voice.

Her pale forehead was creased in a frown. "They felt the vibrations of our passage across *Axismundi*. It's one of their gifts."

I was standing before I even realized I'd had the thought, energy sizzling at my fingertips. "What are they waiting for? We can't just stand here and wait for them to attack." Even to me, my voice sounded a tad on the shrieky side.

Trudy reached out and placed a hand on my wrist, shaking her head. "They won't attack us here. They can't. They'd have to cross the barrier, and they can't do that." She pointed to the ground and, for the first time since arriving in that spot, I noticed the faint green glow extending across the rocky ground. It ran in a fairly straight line, horizontal to the path in both directions, as far as the eye could see.

"Are you sure?" I asked, unwilling to stake our lives on a line of green light.

"As sure as I can be," Trudy told me, releasing my wrist. "When I lived in *Axismundi* we had to come this way a few times, to gather up lost souls who were in danger of crossing into the Tenth. I can assure you the Wraiths won't cross that line."

Brock stared at the creatures for another long moment and then inclined his chin. "We might as well set up camp then. I don't know about the rest of you, but I could use some rest." He and Trudy shared a look that I didn't like at all. But since they followed Deergart back down the path, talking about provisions for the night, I decided to let it rest. I'd broach it with one or the both of them later.

If they were planning on sacrificing themselves for the cause, or something equally stupid and irritating, I was going to go all Middle-Earth-Orc on their butts.

I'd make the Tenth State Wraiths look like church mice in comparison.

A HALF HOUR later I'd spread my sleeping blankets on the ground behind the rock. I believed my aunt that the Wraiths couldn't cross the barrier, but it skeeved me out that they just stood there like that, peering at me with their orange glowing eyes. So, I hid behind the rock. Dropping onto my blankets, I wished for a fan to blow some cool air over my soggy skin. I gave about a second's thought to performing the magic reversal spell and then decided against it.

Maybe my rainbow face would scare the Wraiths away.

Instead, I nearly drained a bottle of water, pouring what I didn't drink over my face to give me a few seconds of relief from the heat. And I managed to eat half of a protein bar before weariness won me over.

I lay back on the blankets, listening to the sounds of the Trolls cooking their evening meal and the soft clank of hammers pounding stakes into the earth for tents, and barely noticed when it all eased away, plunging me into delicious unconsciousness.

THIRTEEN

One of the things about threatening to go full-blown Orc on someone's butt, is you really need to stay awake long enough to do what you've threatened. That's especially important when you suspect that someone is planning something he or she shouldn't be planning.

Because when your weary butt falls into sleep so deep that you begin to suspect someone magicked your water to put you out, the people you planned on giving the verbal smackdown to tend to disappear on you.

"I can't believe you didn't tell me," I yelled at Brock. I wasn't worried about anybody else hearing me screaming like a fish wife because we were standing completely alone in the camp.

I looked around for signs that the Trolls camp had been there and saw nothing.

Not even so much as a hole in the ground where a single stake might have been.

"She knew you wouldn't go for it."

"She was right. This is just wrong. She'll get herself killed."

"No, she won't. It was actually a brilliant plan. Look at the barrier."

I turned my scowl to the area where I'd last seen a line of Wraiths and blinked. Then I squinted, certain that they were there but I hadn't pulled their shapes from the darkness yet.

"They followed Trudy and the Trolls farther up the barrier. They're gone. You and I can slip across the barrier now and, hopefully, find a flower before the Wraiths even know we're here."

"They aren't going to just stand there and watch Trudy stare at them across the barrier. If she's going to keep them interested, she'll need to cross too."

"Maybe," he admitted reluctantly. "But not if we hurry up and get this done. Now, are you ready?"

I was definitely ready to kick some butt. But in that moment it was *his* butt I wanted to kick. He must have read my intention in my expression.

"Don't even think about it, LA..." Brock allowed his demonic form to rise, and he stretched tall and formidable over me. He peered down through fathomless black eyes and let his wings beat the air in warning.

The moving wings sent warm currents of air over my soggy flesh. I almost moaned in pleasure. "I'll give you a week to stop that." With the joke, the tension broke between us and I smiled.

He returned the smile. "Let's go."

We moved to the green barrier, which seemed to ooze from the ground with no discernible source. The magic infusing it was powerful. It caused the small hairs on my body to stand at attention. I tried to read the energy signature but it was incomprehensible. All I could glean from the barrier was a silvery aura that bespoke a Celestial source.

I hesitated, my foot tingling at the idea of stepping past the magic. "Are you sure this won't slice us in half or something when we step over it?"

Brock hesitated just long enough to send my pulse spiking. "Brock?"

His brow furrowed. "Trudy assured me it was passable."

"Just passable? She didn't happen to say it was all roses and cotton candy, did she? A walk in the park? Easy peasy short and squeezy?"

"What does that even mean?"

"I have no idea. I think the energy in this thing is scrambling my brain."

Brock reached out a long, black finger, the claw on the end threatening enough to have me ducking back from his touch.

He hesitated, looked at the claw, and then sighed. "I was just going to point out that the purple has faded a little. You no longer glow in the dark."

"Well, that's reassuring. At least I won't be a beacon for the Wraiths." I took a deep breath and closed my eyes as if not seeing the barrier would help me pass it without suffering instant death.

Then I stepped across.

And agony exploded through me.

Energy sliced up my body like a hot blade, dragging screams from my throat as it severed the flesh of my internal organs like they were tissue paper. I was vaguely aware of slamming into the ground, and then shrieking from the sizzling misery of fire against my skin.

A distant screaming told me Brock was suffering a similar fate. But I couldn't concentrate on helping my friend. I was too busy trying to survive my own adventure with the barrier.

My body pinged off the fiery ground like water off a hot skillet. I slammed again and again into the flames, each touch a combination of misery and relief because at least the energy stopped ripping me to pieces as my body caught fire.

The screaming went on for so long I lost the ability to scream any longer. I was afraid my vocal cords had been sliced away by the restrictive magic, or that the fire consuming me inside and out had melted them away.

I could only lie there and endure the unending torment, praying for a death that never came. Finally, the claws of violence ripping through my insides started to abate. Though intense heat still raked the skin of my back, the flames slowly died out.

My body stopped pinging from flame to blade, and finally collapsed against the heated rocks that formed the surface of the Tenth.

I panted so hard it was making me dizzy. Nausea bloomed in my belly. I lay there for several moments heaving uselessly onto the ground. Sparks flared up around my body, sending tiny flares of clothing into the air like fireworks celebrating my demise.

When the heaves eased, the coughing began. I coughed until I was afraid I was going to cough up a lung.

Or maybe my colon.

Finally, even the coughing stopped. I lay there, a shredded shell of what I'd once been, and wondered why I wasn't lying in a pool of my own blood.

Heavy footsteps shook me out of my daze. I opened my eyes, which were crusty and scratchy from tears that had dried as soon as they emerged. I looked up into the enormous black form rising ten feet above me. I was so exhausted and weak I couldn't even drum up any fear.

I flapped my fingers uselessly. I couldn't even lift my

hand from my chest. "Just eat me and be done with it. I'm cooked. Fork me..."

That didn't sound quite right.

The huge form bent over me and long, muscular arms pulled me off the fiery ground. "Rest, LA. We have to keep moving. You made enough noise to wake the dead."

"Well, excuse me..." I had to stop to lick my dry lips. I was pretty sure all the moisture had been burned from my cells, leaving me flat and dry like a sheet of paper. "You've got some nerve, Mr. Screams-Like-a-Girl."

Brock chuckled. Then he started to run, bobbing me up and down a few times before a surge, the powerful thrust of his wings against the air, and then a peaceful nothingness, and a blessed coolness wafting against my skin.

Eventually, I realized we were flying. I slowly regained my senses and, finally, opened my eyes.

"Don't look down," he told me.

So, of course, I immediately looked down. I gave a terrified little squeal, grabbing hold of his arm and wrapping myself around it like a coat that was two sizes too small. "What the heck?"

"It's cooler up here. I thought you'd appreciate it."

He wasn't wrong. It was blissfully cool. Probably only a hundred degrees. "Okay, I won't argue with you about that. But can we see the flowers from up here?"

"We can see them," he said. "But if we find one we're going to have to land to grab it."

I liked that plan. "So, we only need to land for a quick minute and then take to the air again?" I grinned. "That's perfect. I'm guessing the Wraiths can't fly this high?"

He didn't respond. I looked up at his face, willed him to look at me. "Brock?"

"They can't. But they can fly *that* high." He jerked his chin downward, and I followed his gaze.

What I'd thought was just swirling clouds the first time I looked down wasn't clouds at all. "I guess we're not as high as I thought we were, huh?"

"Unfortunately, no. If we went high enough to stay out of sight, we wouldn't be able to see the flowers."

"Dangit! Nothing's ever easy. So, what's the plan?"

"I'm working on that."

I sighed. As we flew, I watched the ground carefully for a shot of white in the darkness. The sooner we found one of the elusive blooms, the sooner we could grab it and get the heck out of there. As I scanned the ground, I took stock of my condition. "How come I'm not flayed into pieces and charcoaled?" I asked Brock. I'd felt it happening. I couldn't have healed that much damage.

"You weren't flayed and charcoaled. It just felt like it."

"It certainly did. Why?"

He sighed. "Because your body needed to acclimate to the Tenth state. It's a place of death and evil. Living creatures don't just walk into the Tenth. We have to undergo a transformation."

"That's just great. Does this transformation go away when we go back?"

Brock avoided my gaze. "Don't ask me things you don't want to hear the answer to."

Wizard's toes!

I had a thought. "Trudy knew that would happen, didn't she?"

"She did."

I fumed. "Is that the real reason she didn't go through the barrier?"

He peered down at me, a look of pure disgust on his demonic countenance. "Do you really think so little of her?"

I was embarrassed by the affirmative response that flew through my mind. But I shrugged. "She lived in *Axismundi* for much of my life. I don't really know her that well."

He seemed to take that into consideration before answering. Finally, he responded, his voice filled with disapproval. "She knew it would happen. And that you and I would be unable to defend ourselves while the transformation played out. She devised a plan to draw the Wraiths away. To give us time."

I thought about his words for a moment.

"She's already been through the transformation once," Brock said quietly. "It is a blight on her soul that she's sensitive to."

I frowned. "I don't understand. If that's true..."

"Why didn't she insist you stay behind and let her cross instead?"

I frowned that he'd known what I was going to ask. "Yes."

"Would you have stayed behind? Would you have even believed her motives if she'd asked?"

Heat infused my face. I couldn't hold his gaze. I looked away, my gaze falling to the roiling shadows beneath us. "No." I said the word so softly that I wasn't sure how he could have heard me. But he nodded, saying nothing.

I was a jerk. I owed my aunt an apology for believing the worst of her. In that moment, I made a vow that if I survived the current adventure, I'd try harder to understand and bond with Trudy.

The promise came with a strong sense of déjà vu.

I'd made similar promises in the past. Too many times. It seemed I was prone to repeating my mistakes.

"There!" Brock's excited voice brought me out of my unhappy thoughts. I followed the line of his pointing finger. A speck of white glowed through the darkness, drawing us like a beacon to the spot.

Where a veritable army of Wraiths waited to send us crashing to the rocks.

FOURTEEN

"We can't land there," I told him.

"I know." Brock frowned. He stared at the spot as he beat his powerful wings to keep us aloft.

Every throb of his wings reverberated in my chest like a second heartbeat. It was a strange feeling but not entirely unpleasant. "Why don't I draw them off while you grab the flower," I said, mentally cataloging the selection of potions in my pack. I had a couple of things that might drive the Wraiths off long enough for Brock to grab a flower. Though the timing would be tricky. Every potion I brought took a few minutes to prepare.

"Switch that around and you have a good plan."

"No, Brock..."

He shook his head and took off like a shot, away from the flower. "Hey!"

"I'll put you down in a tree. When I've drawn them off, you run as fast as you can to the flower."

"Then what?" I asked. "How are you going to lose them and come back for me?"

He was quiet, so I knew he recognized the flaw in his plan. Finally, he asked, "Okay, then what do you suggest?"

"I have a light potion in my pack. It mimics Angel energy. I'm guessing these jerks don't respond well to light since their world is always dark."

"Go on."

"I'll agree to you drawing them off since you can fly and I can't. Once you've drawn them a ways off, climb to a height where they can't see you and circle back for me. I'll grab the flower and set off the light potion. While they're figuring out how to deal with it, you and I can get away."

"Not a bad plan. But it's going to require very precise timing to work."

"I just need a couple of minutes to prep my spell. If you can figure out a way to slow them down before coming back, that would be best."

He shook his head. "Piece of cake. Good thing you didn't give me the hard part or anything."

I grinned. "Hey, you're welcome."

We dropped three feet straight down, and I squealed, clutching him in sudden terror.

"Air pocket," Brock said with a grin.

I smacked his shoulder, the action hurting me more than it hurt him. "Very funny. There..." I pointed to a tree below us. "Lower me to that tree. I think it's tall enough that the Wraiths won't spot me before you draw them away."

He nodded. "For this to work, I'm going to have to kind of drop you as I do a fly-by."

"What do you mean, kind of drop me?"

I thought I heard an evil chuckle as he opened his arms and let me start to slide away. "Hey!" I rolled out of his arms and frantically grabbed for his massive black paws. Brock closed his fingers over mine.

"Ready?"

"No!"

He released me. "Take care," he whispered, before slamming his wings against the air and shooting off.

At least, that's what I thought he did. I was too busy doing a free fall of about ten feet into the prickly embrace of a dead tree to really notice.

I slammed into the tree, its skeletal branches digging into me like claws and my arms and legs smacking hard against its granite-like trunk. My hands grappled desperately for a hold but I was moving too fast. The impetus of my fall caused several of the limbs I grabbed to break off in my hands.

Finally, something reached out and snagged my pack and I jerked to a painful halt, the sudden loss of movement making my head snap and pain stab through my neck. I hung there for a moment, my feet several feet from the next branch that was strong enough to hold me, and looked around.

The ground below me seemed clear of Wraiths. So that was good anyway.

But I had the new problem of getting down from the tree with my pack.

I could lift my arms and slip free of the pack, hoping I hit a branch below that was strong enough to hold my weight. But I couldn't leave the pack behind, so that wouldn't work.

I was going to have to release myself and catch the pack before I fell. Maybe if I jumped around, the fabric that was stuck on the tree would rip.

Hopefully, nothing important would fall out before I managed to get hold of it again.

"Here goes nothing," I murmured. I lifted my arms and

nothing happened. I wriggled and moved around, trying to release my shoulders from the canvas trap.

I slid a few inches and then stopped, the handle digging painfully into my shoulder.

Then I remembered the knife I'd stuck into my boot. I pulled my legs up and dug inside my leather boot for the handle of the blade.

It wasn't easy. And the pain in my shoulders was excruciating. I gave up for a minute, catching my breath and wriggling to try to release the pressure on my bones. Then I pulled my legs up again and...

The strap slipped free of my shoulder and I suddenly found myself falling. I threw up a hand and made a desperate grab for the pack, but I missed, plunging toward the ground.

Eight feet from the ground, my hip slammed into a thick branch and I bounced off, hitting the trunk of the tree and skimming down the painfully rough bark the rest of the way to the ground. The bark ripped several furrows through my soft underbelly, leaving behind a burning sensation not unlike the fire I'd felt upon crossing the barrier.

I landed with an *umph* and sprawled ungracefully on the gravelly dirt. I lay still for a minute, my breath heaving, and then rolled over and looked up at my trapped pack.

What was I going to do? I didn't have time to climb the tree and try to release it. I'd already wasted most of the allotted couple of minutes.

But without the pack I couldn't make the potion. And without the potion, I was little more than Wraith bait.

"Just perfect," I murmured.

The sweet scent of lily, overlaid with a tinge of cinnamon, filled the air around me. I turned my head and saw the Sweet Death blossom a mere fifteen feet away.

I rolled to my side and took off running. If I couldn't stop the Wraiths with magic, I'd just have to try to outrun them. After all, that had worked so well for me last time.

Ugh.

Maybe I could get out ahead of the pack far enough that Brock could swoop down and scoop me up before they overcame us.

I stopped beside the flower and crouched down, inhaling the sweet scent. It was bigger than it had looked from above, standing a good ten inches tall and as wide across as two of my hands with the fingers spread.

The night shifted, and my head snapped around. I listened carefully for a moment, hearing only my pounding heart and elevated breathing. There was no discernible movement. Nothing that would indicate the Wraiths were returning. But the hairs on the back of my neck were standing on end.

Wrapping my hand around the bloom's base, I tugged.

The flower didn't budge.

I tugged again, harder. Still nothing.

The petals separated and shot me in the face with the stuff that smelled like cinnamon. It stung my skin and made my eyes water profusely. I stepped back and scrubbed at my eyes with my sleeve. "I need to learn not to lead with my face," I murmured grumpily.

A soft breeze whispered past, followed by a whisper of sound. Like a sigh. Or a Wraith moving across the hard ground.

I tried to pry my stinging eyes open to see if something had joined me.

I couldn't see anything but darkness through the shimmering glaze of my tears.

I needed to get moving. Brock was surely going to be

there any second. I scrubbed my sleeve across my eyes again and dropped to my knees. Reaching into my boot, I struggled to grasp the handle of my knife, finding it decidedly easier when I wasn't hanging from the strap of a backpack.

I tugged it out and, keeping my face clear of the fire zone, I sliced through the thick stem of the flower.

A horrendous shriek filled the night. I jumped, surging to my feet, and squinted around me, looking for the source of the scream.

There was no way I didn't know what it was. I'd recognize that eardrum ripping sound anywhere.

A Wraith.

The night exploded into movement in front of me and then stilled. The thing had moved with unnatural speed and then disappeared. I brandished the knife, swinging it from side to side, my watery gaze finding only shadow upon shadow, layered on more shadow.

The glooms split again and the thing came at me, orange eyes flaming and the slit in its belly spreading wide. I threw myself to the side, just in time to avoid being hit with the acidic spit.

The nasty stuff hit the ground where the flower had been and sizzled against the stub still sticking out of the ground, melting it in seconds.

That could have been my skin.

I jumped to my feet and held the knife out as I met the monster's eyes. Even as I did, I knew it was a mistake. A beat later the Wraith was on me. I hit the ground hard with the monster riding my chest and skidded several feet. The Wraith's claw-like hands wrapped around my throat and ended my access to precious, cinnamon-scented air. I fought to release myself from its grip, but I was no match for the Wraith's inhuman strength.

My eyes still stung and watered from the poison in them.

The cinnamon scented poison...

Cinnamon!

I had the flower. Sweet Death for Wraiths.

As my vision started to dim, I fought to lift my hand off the ground where the monster had trapped it. It was no use. The Wraith clearly knew the danger I held, and it was restraining my arm with its leathery form so I couldn't lash out with the lily.

But it wasn't paying any attention to my other arm. I slammed the knife into the monster's side and was rewarded with another painful scream. Its mouth opened and I saw the acidic goo roiling there.

I knew I was seconds away from feeling the melting agony of that acid on my skin. I pulled the knife out and slammed it into the Wraith's side again.

That time, the monster twisted sideways, loosening its grip on my throat and lightening the weight on my arm.

I didn't hesitate.

I lifted the bloom and shoved it into the Wraith's gaping mouth.

The thing shot backward, writhing and screaming as its fiery gaze widened and then dimmed. It twisted and thrashed and shot from side to side, its clawed hands grasping at the air as if trying to pull life from its dense, heat-drenched presence.

The petals of the flower spread outward, filling the cavern and extinguishing the Wraith's fiery spit. As I watched in relief and horror, several seeds spilled from the maw and hit the ground, and then the monster's belly fused shut, and it fell to the ground and went perfectly still.

I shoved to my feet, breathing heavily from fear and lack of oxygen.

Tears filled my eyes as I looked at the melted stump of the flower.

I'd lost the thing that was going to save Deg's life.

We'd have to remain there long enough to find another one. That thought made me clench my teeth against an anguished sob.

The distant sound of massive wings drumming the sky told me Brock was on his way back. I stood there, tears slipping down my cheeks, and realized how disappointed he'd be when he found out how badly I'd muddled things.

But not half as disappointed as I was. I stared at the dead Wraith as the sound of the Demon's wings came closer. Then I shoved the knife into my boot, dried my eyes, and turned back to the tree. I would climb it and try to retrieve my pack.

If Brock and I were going to stay in Tenth state, I was going to need those potions.

But I didn't take a step toward the tree. I skidded to a halt, my eyes going wide.

The ground was no longer dark and rocky.

It had turned white as if snow had found the last circle of Hades.

It was covered in Sweet Death.

FIFTEEN

I've never been so happy to enter *Axismundi* as I was when Brock and I stepped over the barrier again. I'd been gritting my teeth, expecting some version of the effects we'd suffered when entering the Tenth state.

But there was no fiery pain. No claws ripping my insides to mush. Only a slight rumble under my feet that almost sent me to my butt on the rocky ground.

Brock and I halted, glanced at each other, and then shrugged.

"Trudy will be waiting for us at the mouth of the portal, he told me." He grimaced. "Only a two-day walk from here."

My feet ached violently at the thought. "Ugh!" And beneath the dread was a keen awareness that Deg and Littleton lay near death waiting for us to return. I clutched the bulging pack Brock had retrieved from the tree. The almost cloying scent of cinnamon and lilies filled the air around me.

With any luck, we had enough of the magical white

blooms to create anti-Wraith venom for the entire magical population in the Human Realm.

And if we could figure out how to grow the things, we could use the nectar to protect the human population too.

"...a lot less time."

I blinked, dragging my attention back to what Brock was saying. "Sorry, I was thinking. What did you say?"

"I said I could fly us back if you're game. It will take a fraction of the time."

I grinned. "Then what are you waiting for? Let's get Air Brock loaded up and airborne!"

TRUE TO HIS WORD, Brock got us back to the portal in less than a day. It wasn't all champagne and roses though. Riding the Demon's back as if he were a dragon was stressful. I held on for dear life through twists and turns and air pockets, some of which I swore were manufactured by the Demon because they always seemed to happen just when I'd managed to doze off for a little nap.

Finally, after going well out of our way to avoid a wandering flock of screeching Harpies, whose rotted-meat stench extended well beyond their gaggling group, Brock pointed toward the ground, where the passage between realms opened out into a familiar clearing.

As usual, the light was poor, but the soft green illumination oozing from the pores of Axismundi soil illuminated several forms thrashing about in the space.

I quickly recognized the blocky shapes of Deergart's Trolls. They seemed to be doing some kind of dance.

Then I saw the smaller forms and realized they weren't dancing. They were fighting. "Brock!"

He nodded. "I see them. Hold on."

I barely had time to groan–I'd learned to hate those two words over the last several hours–before he tilted violently and rode an air current into a sharp turn.

"I'll set us down in those trees over there. We'll have to sneak up on them."

I nodded, though Brock wouldn't see it, and tugged my pack around. "I think I have a cloaking spell left in here..."

Five minutes later, Brock and I were skulking along the path, listening to the clank of swords as the Trolls did battle with a small force of humanoid *Axismundis* and a handful of what I recognized were prison catacomb guards.

Brock had sloughed off his demonic form so my cloaking magic would work on him and he was carrying a short sword he'd been wearing in a sheath across his chest.

We stopped at the edge of the clearing and I settled my pack to the ground.

Brock looked at me as I pulled my knife from my boot, and I nodded.

We moved into the clearing, our steps light and fast. We needn't have bothered with stealth. The battle was loud and brisk. Nobody was paying attention to us.

Brock moved up behind a Demon guard and wrapped an arm around his throat from behind, placing his blade just under the creature's scaly chin. "Drop the weapon."

The guard stiffened, his sword held across his body to capture the strikes of the bleeding Troll he was battling, and the Troll gave the inferior metal a bone-jarring slash with his Troll blade, breaking it into pieces. Then he moved forward, the tip of his blade digging into the guard's leather-like chest. "Kneel, fool," the Troll growled.

Brock stepped away and headed to the next altercation.

I spied Deergart at the edge of the clearing. He was

back on his heels and bleeding profusely. The Troll had his blade in defensive mode and was backtracking as a massive humanoid performed a series of lightning-fast slashing maneuvers.

While I watched in horror, the *Axismundi* soldier struck a vicious blow to Deergart's rocklike form. The Troll leader fell to his knees.

The soldier lifted his blade and Deergart stared up at him, refusing to look away as he awaited death.

"No!" I screamed, drawing confused glances from several nearby attackers. My cloaking magic slipped away as I started to run. I had to get to the Troll before that blade came down and ended him.

But I wasn't going to make it. "Hey!" I yelled at the soldier standing over Deergart.

He didn't hear me.

"Hey, stupid!" I tried again.

He slowly turned his head, only to offer me an evil smile. And then I watched in horror as his arm slashed downward.

The last thing I saw as my feet left the ground was Deergart's sad eyes, closing in expectation of death.

I slammed into the soldier just as the blade found the Troll. A pain-filled scream filled the area and blood flew, splashing warmly over me.

Hitting the ground and rolling, I pulled the heavy form of the attacking soldier with me. I spun to my knees and looked down, finding my blade pressed against the soldier's throat.

His eyes were wide, filled with terror. His heartbeat pounded between us, fast and hard. I could almost taste his fear.

With the memory of Deergart's last expression uppermost in my mind, my rage made me relish that fear. My hand tightened on the handle of the blade. I fought the desire to press it slowly into the soft flesh. I swallowed hard as the craving turned to pleasure. Pain pulsed through my mind.

A warning.

I forced my fingers to loosen on the handle and pulled air into my lungs, battling the urge to kill. I couldn't let their lack of compassion and lust for murder infect me.

I was better than that.

The urge slid through me again. A little voice inside my head prodded me to do it. Removing one more evil Demon from the worlds was a good thing, I told myself. One less blood-thirsty monster to fight off later.

But how was that better, if killing him only created another blood-thirsty monster? One that wore the face of a Familiar?

I wasn't a monster. I was a healer. One of the good guys. Wasn't I?

Then why was I licking my lips in anticipation of cutting through his throat and watching his blood stain the ground?

A heavy hand fell on my shoulder, and I twitched under the gentle touch.

"Let it be, LeeAnn," a gravelly voice said. "It's not your place. You're not a soldier."

Tears burned my eyes, and the blood-lust eased away. I turned my head and looked up at Deergart, bleeding from a deep gash in one arm, but whole and alive. "You're okay."

He bobbed his boulder-like head, the sparse covering of light brown hair dancing with the movement. "Thanks to you." He frowned. "If you kill that man, I'll carry it for the rest of my life. Not because he died. He deserves to die. But because my carelessness will have resulted in you claiming a stain on your soul."

I shook my head. "This isn't on you."

"Yes. It is." He held out a blocky hand. "Come. Let me do what needs to be done."

I glanced down at the man beneath me, my lips thinning with regret. Then I shoved the dregs of rage away and gave Deergart my hand, letting him pull me off the ground.

The man I'd taken down tried to leap off the ground. He met the business end of Deergart's boot to the head for his efforts, collapsing bonelessly back to the ground.

Deergart grinned. "Now that felt good."

I laughed.

Brock wandered over. "All good here?"

I nodded, watching as Deergart bound the man's wrists and tugged him over his good shoulder. "We'll take him back with us. The council will have questions."

Brock and I shared a look. There was a question in his gaze...speculation. I'd have loved to ask him what he was thinking, but we had other business to discuss. He turned to Deergart. "One of your men told me they took Trudy."

Deergart winced. "Took is a strong word. She more or less just left with them."

I frowned. "Did she say anything before she left?"

"She told me to defeat the soldiers and carry the news back to the council."

"Your man also said he overheard her discussing a bounty on LA's head."

I felt my eyes go wide. "On me? Why?"

"He didn't know. But he said Trudy left with them shortly afterward," Brock responded.

I looked at the Troll leader. "Did she tell you why she was leaving? Did they threaten her?"

Deergart shrugged. "Not that I could tell. She didn't divulge what she was doing. I wish she had. I doubt she'd want me to report what I believe really happened here."

"What do you think happened?" Brock asked, frowning.

The Troll looked me right in the eye, his expression unhappy. "I think your aunt just sold us out for a return to power in *Axismundi*."

Pain sliced through me. "Are you sure? Maybe you misinterpreted what you saw, Deergart."

He shrugged, wincing, and placed a hand protectively over his wounded shoulder. "I wish I could believe that, LA. But the guy she left with wasn't using force. She didn't even look upset."

As much as I wanted to cling to hope, I'd feared just such an outcome from the moment Trudy returned to the Human Realm. There was something just a little bit off about her. Something I couldn't quite trust.

I'd told myself the problem was mine. I had trouble trusting. And her actions since we'd reunited had been unpredictable at best. But hope can only take you so far. And Deergart hadn't suffered my doubts about Trudy. His read on her betrayal had more weight than my wish for it not to be true. "Okay. Then we'd better get back and see what we can do to help our people."

"Then we need to prepare for whatever's coming," Brock said on a frown. "Because if Trudy's working a plan against us that includes siccing Wraiths on our butts, we're in even more trouble than we thought. And that's saying something."

SIXTEEN

The return trip through the portal seemed to take twice as long as it had when we'd entered *Underworld*. I was keenly aware of how dire Deg's condition had been when we left. We'd been gone four days by my assessment, and I was terrified I'd lose him before we made it back.

My mood was black because of my aunt's betrayal. I didn't relish telling my mother that her sister had thrown us over again for her own interests. She'd trusted Trudy and would feel her betrayal keenly.

But I couldn't focus on that at the moment. I had the cure we needed to help my Witch and Littleton. Getting them that help needed to be my first priority.

Unfortunately, the long trek through the portal passageway gave me way too much time to think and worry.

We finally stepped out of the passage in *Illusory Park*. It was nighttime there, and brutally cold after the heat of Axismundi and the passage. But I welcomed the cold. The claustrophobic heat we'd left behind had marked me in a way I wouldn't soon forget.

"Mandy will pick us up at the central point," Brock told

me, slipping his phone back into his pocket. "She said Deg's still hanging on."

Relief coursed through me, making it easier to breathe. "Thank goodness. Let's hope she can do something with these flowers before he gets worse."

Despite Brock's reassurance, it wasn't Mandy who met us in the park. Oscar stepped out of the *Familiar, Inc.* van when we came out of the trees. He looked even more harried than usual. "We need to hurry. Littleton's taken a turn. Mandy needs those blooms ASAP."

The drive to the office took forever. I sat on the edge of my seat, foot drumming nervously on the floorboard, as Oscar moved the van efficiently—but much too slowly for my taste—through the heavy traffic on the main road.

The van had barely rocked to a stop when I jumped out, shoving through the double glass front doors and running toward the elevator.

I didn't wait for Oscar and his special key. I took the steps to the fourth level and ran toward the glass doors of the clinic. Mandy was waiting for me just inside. I practically threw the pack at her. "They're in there."

She turned and started toward the rooms at the back. "You got more than one bloom?"

"Several, actually."

"Good. I have no idea how this is going to work."

I followed her into the second room and jolted to a stop as I spotted Littleton. He was so white I couldn't tell where his skin started and the sheet ended. He looked as if he'd shrunk since being hit by the Wraiths. He barely made a bump beneath the covers.

His dark hair was lank and stringy with sweat, and his handsome features wore a sheen of perspiration. Even his lips were gray. He twitched constantly in his sleep, his eyes moving ceaselessly under the lids. As I watched, his hands shot into the air and the fingers clenched, though I didn't know if it was from pain or from the nightmares he was clearly having.

He was a man fighting more than one battle, and he appeared to be losing them both. "He looks horrible," I whispered to Mandy.

She threw me a glare. "We have work to do. Grab that mortar and pestle over there."

I did as she asked, taking the petals she handed me and dropping them into the stone dish.

"Grind those until they're a fine paste. And hurry."

I ground furiously while Mandy wove a spell above Littleton's head. It was the most complex spell I'd ever seen. I had no idea its purpose or origin. "What is that?"

She glanced my way. "You don't want to know."

Which meant she'd used elements of dark magic in the spell.

"Littleton is a Dark Elf, so the healers and I decided we needed to include the black arts in his cure."

"Blood?" I asked, wincing.

"Freely given," she said snottily. "Though under duress, which means the appropriate stress points are there." She tied off the spell and turned to me. "Are you done?"

I handed her the mortar. She flung me a look and then reached into her pocket, pulling out a small vial filled with thick, red liquid.

Blood.

She opened it and let three drops fall into the mortar, then held her hand flat over the concoction, fingers splayed and eyes closed as she spoke the spell.

She dipped her finger into the blood and flower mixture and scooped some of it out. Pressing her finger against

Littleton's lips, she worked the mixture into his mouth. Then, with her other hand, Mandy touched the central point of her spell and sent energy into it. Pale pink magic burst at the center of the spell and spread through its many strands, sparking on the air whenever it touched a juncture in the weave. The magic hit the beginning and end points at the same time and fire burst on the air, leaving behind a fine mist of light gray ash that filtered down and coated Littleton.

He immediately stopped twitching. His eyes stilled behind his lids, and he sighed softly, seeming to relax into sleep.

Mandy staggered backward, one hand wiping her brow. I suddenly saw what I hadn't seen when I'd come through the door. She was dead on her feet.

I had no doubt she'd been at the two men's bedsides since we'd left. It was doubtful she'd gotten any rest at all.

I grabbed the mortar from her hand and wrapped an arm around her waist to support her. "You need to rest."

Mandy shook her head, her dark hair swinging limply with the motion. Her weariness was complete, showing in the pastiness of her usually rosy complexion and the lankness of her generally glossy, shoulder-length hair. "You're not going to do anybody any good if you collapse," I told her.

"I'll be fine. I just need to..." I helped her to the chair beside Littleton's bed. "—sit for a few minutes."

She closed her eyes, leaning her head back against the chair back. "Just rest a few..."

She fell almost instantly asleep. I settled the mortar on the table beside Littleton's bed and went to find a healer.

I'd try to mimic Mandy's spell to help Deg. And if I

couldn't get it done with another healer's help, then I'd wake Mandy up.

But I hoped I wouldn't have to do that.

Brock was waiting in the outer room when I came out. "Is he okay?"

I scrubbed a hand over my face, weariness finding me as the adrenaline bled away. "I don't know. He seems more comfortable. We'll just need to give it time."

Brock nodded. "Mandy?" There was something in his expression when he asked. Something I'd noticed growing stronger by the day. The Demon was fond of the Witch. Overly fond. I didn't want him to get hurt. Mandy was a hard one. She might not worry about his feelings if he was overstepping.

But it wasn't my place to interfere. Brock was a grown... erm...Demon. He could take care of himself. And I figured that included managing his own love life.

"Exhausted. She's sleeping. If I can help Deg without her, I will. If not, we'll have to wake her up."

He nodded. "I'll go have one of her special vitamin shakes made up. It will help her regain some energy to get her through another healing."

"Thanks, Demon."

His smile was tired but filled with affection. And maybe just a smidge of pity. He no doubt felt sorry for me that my aunt was such a scoundrel. I didn't want his pity. I planned to deal with Trudy myself. In my own way. But not until I knew Deg and Littleton would be okay.

Brock left and I turned toward Deg's room. I was half afraid to go in there for fear he'd look like Littleton had. Or worse.

I didn't want to see my Witch looking like a frail version of himself. In my current state, it just might be my undoing.

I pulled air into my lungs and expelled it, then started toward his room.

The outer door opened and closed behind me with a soft snick. I turned, thinking it was one of the healers. "Good. You're here. We need to administer the anti-toxin to Deg..."

My words choked off as I turned and saw who'd come into the clinic.

"Hello, LA."

The Nephilim was over two hundred years old and looked about fourteen. The Nephilim was over two hundred years old and looked about fourteen. The product of an Angel father and a Familiar mother, Mabel and her two brothers could shift into feline form—kittens because of their youth—and easily straddle the boundaries between the Human and Celestial Realms.

I'd known the three as kittens initially, and hadn't realized until recently that my adorable charges were actually very powerful Nephilim sent to keep an eye on things in the Human Realm.

Mabel's pretty face was taut with concern. She hurried over and pulled me into a hug. "How is he?"

I returned the hug, feeling soothing magic sliding over me as the Nephilim's energy embraced me. "He's still unconscious. Brock and I went to the Tenth and brought back some flowers..."

"*Dulcemori*?" Mabel asked, pulling back to look me in the eye.

I nodded.

She stared at me for a long moment, as if waiting for me to tell her the rest. But I wasn't ready to talk about my duplicitous aunt. "Littleton was attacked too. He's in worse shape. But Mandy and I got the potion into him. He seemed better when I left."

She inclined her head. "That's good. I came as soon as I heard."

She watched me carefully, and I couldn't help wondering why. Did I look that bad? "Thanks," I said, my voice breaking. "I'm not sure there's anything anybody can do."

"I wanted to be here with you. And..." her voice changed, strained with warning, "I have news."

From the look on her face and her tone, I was pretty sure I wasn't going to like her news. "Oh?"

The clinic door opened and my mother strode through, followed by a stern-faced Oscar.

Just for fun, I threw him a glare.

Mother strode over and stopped in front of my friend. "Hello, Mabel. How are things in the Celestial Realm?"

Mabel performed a graceful curtsy that, on anybody else, would have seemed strangely out of place. She ducked her head, the silky blonde curls that fell to her shoulders dropping down to obscure her expression. "Madam Queen."

Mother fluttered her fingers impatiently. "You can just call me Katherine. I've given up the crown."

Mabel glanced my way. I let my eyes widen to let her know I'd been just as surprised by the change as she seemed to be. "Katherine. I came with news you need to hear."

Mother indicated a seating area near the door, but Mabel shook her head. "I won't keep you. LeeAnn has more healing to do. But it's imperative you know what's going on."

That sounded pretty good to me. Mostly I'd spent the

last few days not knowing any of what was going on until it bit me on the derriere.

"Go on," Mother said. I noted the tension firming her lips and the way she twined her hands together in front of her. I'd learned long ago that meant she was bracing for something. Did she already know what Mabel was going to say?

"You've spoken to Tollman?"

I blinked in surprise. Of all the directions the conversation could have gone, that would have been my last guess.

Mother glanced at me and then nodded.

Mabel sighed. "It's been verified. His name's Anthrall. He went off our radar almost a year ago, and there hasn't been a peep since. The only sign we have that he's here is the dead reporter and...what Tollman found entangled in the man's soul."

Mother clasped her hands and looked down at the floor, her expression taut.

I waved at Mabel. "Hello?"

Looking perplexed, she gave me a finger wave back. "Um. Hi?"

Heaving an exasperated sigh, I clarified, "I have no idea what you're talking about. I've been in *Axismundi*."

"Oh. I'm sorry, LA." She shook her head, her pretty face tightening. "I'm afraid we know who's behind the Wraith attacks."

"This Anthrall guy?" I asked.

She nodded. "He's found a way to get them out of the Tenth."

"How's he doing it?" Mother asked. Her lips were pinched so tight they'd turned white.

"Soul riding."

"Explain," Mother demanded.

Mabel's gaze rolled skyward as if she were looking for direction from the heavens. She was probably just gathering her thoughts. She couldn't be enjoying the current discussion. If someone had figured out how to break the worst of the worst souls out of Hell, that was a huge mark against the gatekeepers in the Celestial Realm. "He's discovered that he can insert—it's a terrible word, but it's the best one we can come up with—them into the newly or nearly dead. Or living souls who've been altered by the physics of the Tenth."

I let that roll over me for a moment and then it punched me in the gut. I made a startled noise, my hand slamming over my mouth as my skin tried to crawl off my body. I stumbled backward, my hands rubbing frantically along my arms, where all the hair was standing on end.

"LeeAnn?" my mother asked with a worried glance. "What's wrong?"

I clamped my lips together and gave my head a quick shake. My eyes felt as if they might pop out of my head. "It just sounds awful," I wrenched out through stiff lips.

Mother gave an impatient sigh. But when my gaze met Mabel's, her eyes were narrowed with speculation.

"Do you know how many he's managed to break out?" I asked to distract the Nephilim.

"No. How many of them did you and Deg see at The Guild headquarters?"

"I don't know, maybe a dozen."

She sighed. "We can assume the number is at least double that. However, there's no reason to believe he's stopped transporting them. Souls die every day..." She let that slide through the room, her implication clear. Hundreds of thousands of humans died every day. Even if he could access only a tiny fraction of that, we were talking about terrifying odds. "We'll be overrun. These things aren't easy to kill."

Mabel nodded, looking as worried as I felt.

"This Anthrall guy's directing them?" I asked.

"Yes."

"Do we know what his ultimate plan is?"

Mabel shook her head. "Not the specifics, but I think we can guess the general goal."

"To gain control of the realm that has the most latent energy and natural resources of any of the twelve realms," Mother said.

"Yes."

"So, who is this guy?" I asked. "How is he able to do this?"

"Anthrall was the Celestial Realm's guardian for the Tenth. He's been the controller there for millennia. He's in charge of selecting souls as well as managing the barrier and other restrictive measures."

"Like Sweet Death," I murmured.

"Exactly. He was in a perfect position to figure out how to break all the controls."

"If he works for the Celestial Realm," I began.

"He's an Angel," Mabel verified softly.

My stomach twisted with alarm. "Freakin' fantastic." That would explain why Tollman had run like a sissy girl from Becksmart's office.

"Yes," Mabel said in monumentally understated agreement.

"What's his connection to The Guild?" Mother asked. "Do you think they helped him?"

"*That*, I can't tell you. If you can find out, it would be very helpful."

Mother looked at me.

"Let me take care of Deg first. Then Brock and I can try to get to the bottom of it."

Mother nodded. "Take Trudy with you."

My stomach sank. I really didn't want to have the Trudy conversation with my mother. But it wasn't fair to keep her in the dark. I decided on a half-truth instead, telling myself that I'd make it up to her later. When the world didn't feel like it was ending. "Um. Trudy stayed behind in *Axismundi*."

Mother's face paled. "She what?"

"Yeah, she's working some of her relationships there, trying to get information about what's going on. She promised she'll be right behind us though."

Mother nodded, but she was frowning. I knew if I didn't get out of there soon, she'd be back at me, prodding me until she got the truth. I quickly excused myself and went to see my Witch.

At least I knew what I could do to help Deg. I had no idea how to make it better for my mother when she found out her sister had betrayed us yet again.

SEVENTEEN

"How are we going to do this?" Brock asked.

I glanced over and saw the lines of weariness in his face. I knew how he felt. I'd passed empty in my energy stores a while back. I handed him a protein bar. "We need to reach Tollman. He knows how to find Graham Cullpepper."

"Who's that?"

Oh yeah, I'd forgotten Brock hadn't been with Deg and me when we'd tracked down the leader of The Guild. I pushed thoughts of Deg away because, if I let myself remember how pale and sickly he'd looked when I left him, I wouldn't have it in me to do what we needed to do. "He's the leader of The Guild. And a truly reprehensible human being." As I said the words, I wondered if they were true. Not the part about being reprehensible. He was that and more. But did I really know if he was human? "Tollman will know," I murmured.

"He'll know what?" Brock turned the steering wheel, and his big truck bumped over patchy ice and snow toward the center of town.

"He'll know whether Cullpepper's human. Deg and I

assumed he was. But given the fact that we have a rogue Angel hiding somewhere in *Illusion City*, we can't take anything for granted."

Brock tucked the last bite of his bar into his mouth and chewed thoughtfully. He'd been unusually quiet since we'd learned what we were dealing with. I had to assume he was worried about dealing with a rogue Angel.

Heaven knew I certainly was. That kind of power... I shook off my dire thoughts and dialed Tollman. It rang several times before I finally hung up. He was avoiding us, and I had to wonder why. Did he know something about Anthrall he didn't want to share? Or was it a simple case of "us against them" mentality? I certainly hoped not.

The last thing we needed was to deal with two of the powerful supernaturals.

"What about Mabel?" Brock asked.

"Hmm?" I stared straight ahead, lost in my thoughts. I needed to figure out where Tollman was and get to him. Something told me he was the only one who could help us.

"Mabel. She's a Nephilim. She must have some power that will help with a low-level Angel."

I nodded. "She'll be there if we need her." If there was one thing I'd figured out about Celestial beings, it was that they didn't follow anybody's plan but their own. They didn't come when they were called, and they didn't sit or stay either. Everything was orchestrated to suit themselves.

Tollman was a perfect example of that. I thought about the times we'd encountered him. The way he'd always shown up when there was a problem that needed to be solved. The way he'd trusted Deg and me to help.

He had to be really upset about Littleton. They'd become good friends in a short time. Which made sense, because they were arguably two of the most powerful magic users in the Human Realm.

I blinked as a sudden thought sifted through my brain. "I know where he is."

Brock glanced my way, frowning. "Who?"

"Tollman. I know where he is. Turn around. And hurry. He might not wait around much longer."

THE WARM COZINESS of my home wrapped around me as I came through the front door. I stopped just inside and inhaled deeply, closing my eyes at the welcoming scent of my herbs and potions.

Something shifted in my chest, and my eyes shot open. For a brief moment I smelled the stench of sulfur above the sweet smell of lavender, rosebud, and mint.

Someone was in my home.

I pulled energy to my fingertips and let it dance there, ready to throw at whatever had invaded my space. Behind me, Brock stiffened, immediately aware of the new tension in the air. "What is it?"

"Somebody's here."

"Yeah? You expected him to be here, right?"

It was a reasonable question. We *had* returned to my home because my instincts told me it was where Tollman would be. But what I'd felt hadn't been Celestial energy. It had been darker. Much darker. Like a piece of hell had broken off inside my head. I moved quickly and silently into the kitchen and stopped at the door, the magic flaring as alarm spread through me.

He sat at the small, round table, his back to the door. His head was bowed, the untidy dark brown locks even more unruly than usual. His trademark button-down shirt was rumpled and torn, the tails untucked and trapped by the slats of the chair back. His long legs stretched out before him, the cuffs of his slacks filthy and a puddle of melted snow beneath them. His hands rested on his thighs, fisted, the knuckles white.

He didn't look up when we entered.

"Tollman?"

His head remained bowed. He stayed silent.

I stopped beside him and let the energy leach away from my hands. I reached out and touched his shoulder. The muscle beneath my fingers was rock hard. I knew he was strong, but I was pretty sure what I was feeling was pure tension. A vein pulsed in his throat, and his jaw flexed underneath some strong emotion. "What is it?"

Tollman slowly lifted his navy gaze to mine. "I couldn't do it."

I frowned, glancing toward Brock. I jerked my head toward the sink. He nodded, heading over to get the distraught Angel a glass of water.

I lowered myself into the chair across from Tollman.

"What couldn't you do?" I asked softly.

He shook his head. "I couldn't do what needed to be done. He's out of control. I should have taken him down."

My chest tightened. If he was telling me what I thought he was telling me, we were in deep trouble. I took a leap. "Anthrall?"

He twitched, his gaze sharpening. "You know?"

I nodded. "Mabel told us."

His forearms tightened, chorded muscle bulging along their length. "He's..." He swallowed hard. "He *was* my friend. I couldn't take him down."

Brock handed him a glass of water and he took it,

downing most of it in one long, drink. He nodded at the Demon and settled the glass onto the table. "I'm sorry. I've let you down."

"No. You haven't." I leaned closer. "Unless you're telling me you won't help us stop this before more humans are killed."

He held my gaze for a long moment. I started to panic, worried that was exactly what he was telling me. "Tollman?"

He sighed. "No. I'm not telling you that. I'll help you. It needs to be done."

"Good." Glancing at Brock, I noted the relief sliding through his weary gaze. I pushed to my feet. "I'll make tea. I might have some cookies around here somewhere too. We'll refill our energy stores. Then we need to make a plan to take this guy and his Wraiths down." I looked at Tollman, and he slowly nodded.

As I walked away from the table, Brock eased his long body into the chair I'd left. A moment later he started to ask the Angel questions. To my great relief, Tollman answered them with satisfactory detail.

"Do you know where he is now?"

Tollman shook his head. "No. But I can find him."

"That's good," I said as I settled the teapot onto the stove.

"Not really. He's gone to ground and surrounded himself with his nasty pets," Tollman growled out.

I grimaced. "How many of them?" I asked.

"Too many." Tollman scrubbed a big hand over his prickly jaw.

"What's Anthrall's connection to the Sensitives of The Guild?" Brock asked. "Are they helping him?"

Tollman didn't answer for a long moment. I settled a

cup of tea and a plate of cookies in front of him and waited, hands on hips, for him to respond. As silence continued between us, I fixed him with an unwavering stare that eventually brought his gaze to mine. "I'm sorry."

Frustration filled me as I misinterpreted his response. "You told us you'd help. We're counting on you, Angel."

He shook his head.

Something dark twisted inside me, and I'd pulled energy into my hand and wrapped my fingers around his muscular throat before I even realized what I was doing.

Brock stood up so fast his chair flew backward. He grabbed for me, paling. "LA!"

"Don't!" I shot him a glare that made him hesitate, his face going slack with shock.

Tollman didn't flinch. He didn't try to get away, even as my magic burned into his skin, sending the stench of burning flesh into the air. His gaze never wavered from mine. Sadness filled his navy eyes, and the fine lines around his eyes and mouth deepened. "I'm so sorry."

"What, Tollman?" I growled out. "What are you sorry about? Why won't you help us?"

He reached up and wrapped a hand around my fingers, pulling them easily from his throat.

I should have felt guilty about the bands of burned tissue on his throat as I stepped back. Instead, I felt a perverse kind of pleasure at the sight.

The Angel was working against us. That was unacceptable. "You were sent here to help the humans. You're supposed to protect them."

"Yes," he whispered.

Eyeing me as if I might explode into a ravening monster, Brock picked up his chair and eased himself back into it. "Look, man," he said, his gaze still on me, "you need to give us something. As you can tell, we're just about out of patience."

When I slid a glare to the Demon, he lifted his midnight brows.

I got the message. I was overreacting. I'd gone too far. I pulled air into my lungs and held it, working to calm my nerves and send my magic back to the place where it waited for me to call it. After a few beats I felt much calmer. Still, just to be safe, I was going to switch out my caffeinated tea for something more soothing.

Like chamomile. Or Valium. "Sorry," I mumbled to no one in particular.

Brock grabbed a cookie off the plate and stuffed it in his mouth. Probably so he wouldn't say something snarky that might get him killed.

"What I meant," Tollman ground out through gritted teeth, "was that I was sorry for lying to you."

I stopped pouring water into my mug and looked at him. "Lying? About what?"

"Cullpepper."

I glanced at Brock, his brows peaked again.

"What about him," I asked as I finished pouring the water.

"He's not what he appears."

I knew it! "He's not human?"

Tollman shook his head. "Not even a little."

I stopped pouring. "How long have you known?"

"Not long. A few days." He shifted in his chair, his gaze not meeting mine.

I bit back an enraged response. A few days might have made a lot of difference.

"So, who or *what* is he?" Brock asked.

"He's been called many things," Tollman said enigmatically.

I felt irritation starting to rise again.

Brock must have noticed. He lifted a hand to warn me off.

"He's been called The Guardian, The Warden, and The Keeper."

I sipped my tea and set it down on the counter, leaning back and crossing my arms so I wouldn't be tempted to tweak him with an energy arrow. "How about we just call him Anthrall?"

Tollman looked disappointed that I knew. I cocked my head and lifted my brows. "You couldn't just say that?"

"I was trying to..."

"It's like talking to a teenaged girl. Yeesh! Is everybody in your realm such a drama mama?"

He shrugged, leaving me with the impression that they probably were.

"Okay, so your buddy, Anthrall, wants to take over the Human Realm. He found a way to bring his—pets—as you call them, through the portal."

Brock frowned.

"And then what?'

"He used the reporter to spread rumors of magic to distract you while he put his plan into place."

"Except it didn't completely work," Brock said. "Why?"

"Because, when he killed Becksmart..."

I held up a hand, interrupting him. "Why *did* he kill the reporter?"

"Probably because he talked too much. But I'm sure Anthrall also saw an opportunity to create chaos in the magical world. If Littleton had fought back..."

"The world would have seen magic in action and been afraid," Brock finished for him.

"So why draw us to headquarters? Why send his Wraiths to attack Littleton and Deg?" I couldn't shake the idea that Tollman might have had something to do with the attacks. I watched him carefully, waiting for his response.

Tollman looked sad. "Who knows what's on his mind? He's crazed with power and greed. He sees an opportunity to rule the twelve dimensions from here and he'll do anything to gain that power."

"I repeat my earlier question," Brock said, "Why didn't Anthrall's plan work? How did you discover he was here?"

"We got lucky," Tollman said, wincing as if it weren't luck at all. "He didn't plan on LA's unique power being used on the reporter, or on my being there to read the magic she pulled from the corpse."

"You knew it was him," I said. "That's why you ran off like you did."

He had the good grace to look embarrassed. "I had to be sure before I..."

"Before you what?" Brock asked in a decidedly hostile tone. "Before you came to us and told us what was going on? Oh, that's right, you *didn't* come to us, did you? We've been chasing our tails all over the twelve realms, trying to figure out how to fight those Wraiths. And now we find out you could have already stopped this."

I realized Brock was right. If Anthrall was driving the Wraiths... "You could have stopped him. Ended him. And the Wraiths would have been weakened. We could have defeated them with normal magic."

Tollman didn't try to defend himself. He just sat there looking miserable.

I felt no pity for him. "My friends are dying because

you did nothing." I walked over and leaned down, forcing him to look at me. "*Your* friend is dying. Littleton may not recover. That's on you, Angel."

To my shock, he simply nodded. "I know that better than you realize. And I'll have to live with it the rest of my long, long existence if those men die. But that's why I finally came to you. I'm prepared to do what needs to be done. I'm ready to form a plan to stop him."

EIGHTEEN

While we waited for Mandy, my mother, and a select few members of the council to come to us—Tollman had insisted the meeting take place at my house because he feared Anthrall had a friend at *Familiar, Inc.*—I went out to the sanctuary and spent some time doing mundane chores and visiting with the cats who'd chosen to stay with me for a while. The activity soothed and centered me again.

I'd been anxious about my guests while I'd been gone. It was reassuring to find them fat and glossy with health and enjoying the controlled environment. Though they could come and go as they wished, many of the cats who sought refuge in my sanctuary had suffered from the cruel temps outside or were recovering from illness or injury. Fortunately, I had none with medical needs at the moment, or I'd have had to bring someone in from Familiar, Inc. to tend to them while I'd been in *Axismundi*. I'd left them plenty of food, and the pond offered an endless supply of clean water. The carefully constructed ecosystem offered warmth and protection. In short, it was everything an unfettered cat could ever want.

I'd been there almost an hour when Brock came to tell me the others had arrived. I was sitting on a rock in the center of the space, the surface warm from a golden beam of sunshine that had found its way through the steel gray cloud cover overhead. I was staring into the small rock pond I'd magicked nearby and listening to the water sigh happily as it slid down the rocky incline and back into the pool at its base.

I'd used the time to attempt communication with Celeste and had not been successful. I was really getting worried. Grandmama Celeste had never gone so long without communicating with me. And she'd definitely never ignored so many direct requests to visit with her. Especially since she'd gone to the *Elysian Fields.* She'd seemed hungry for news of the people and work she'd loved while alive. If someone had told me she'd deliberately go incommunicado, I'd have laughed. But if that wasn't what was happening, I didn't want to consider the alternative.

Brock reached down and scratched behind the pert white-tipped ears of the black tomcat in my lap. I would have liked to believe the big tom was there to cuddle with me. But I suspected he'd simply been craving the warmth of the sunbeam, and I'd been in his way. The tomcat apparently decided to use me like a bumpy feline couch.

"They're here," Brock said in a tired voice.

I nodded but didn't move. Sitting down in the sun had been a big mistake. As a Familiar who shifted into her own cat when absolutely necessary, I had just enough feline in me to make me want to curl up in that sunbeam and lose myself in a day or two of sleep.

"LA?"

I sighed. "I'm coming."

"No. I wanted to ask..."

When he hesitated I looked up, a question in my gaze.

"In there. When you lost it on the Angel and used your magic against him..."

I winced. "Crazy, huh? I don't know what came over me." Whatever it was, it had come over me a lot recently.

He shoved his hands into the pockets of his jeans. "That's just it...when you did that...your eyes..."

I waited, dread of what he would say curling in my belly like a fist. Something dark had been hunkered deep in my core since we'd left the Tenth behind. I suspected it was that stain Brock had mentioned Trudy suffering. I wondered if he felt it too.

A moment later, Brock seemed to lose interest in asking his question. Shrugging, he said, "We should probably get in there."

MANDY HURRIED over as we came into the kitchen. She was smiling and pulled me into an unaccustomed hug. "He's okay. Deg is okay."

Tears burned my eyes as I hugged her back. "Thank goodness," I murmured, sniffling as the tears slid down my cheeks. I glanced at Tollman and he inclined his chin, looking relieved.

"And Littleton?" he asked, his voice gruff.

Mandy's smile dimmed. "Too soon to tell. If he's not better by tomorrow, we've decided to use a stronger potion."

If they'd used blood magic the first time, I couldn't imagine what she'd consider stronger. And I was pretty sure I didn't want to know.

Mother walked over and squeezed my hand. "You saved him." She grasped Brock's hand too. "Both of you."

I nodded, laughing happily. "What a relief."

"He was chomping at the bit to come with," Mandy said, chuckling huskily. "We almost had to strap him down to keep him there."

"Then he's definitely feeling better," I agreed.

"He's a Witch. Of course he wants to contribute," a sour voice said behind me. I heard the sound of thick heels clacking aggressively against my kitchen floor.

I turned to find Serena, high priestess of Deg and Mandy's coven, gliding my way. Her cold, black gaze slid over Mandy and landed on me, her thin lips curling with distaste. "But I'll give you and the Demon your due. I'm certain gathering those blooms can't have been easy."

I nearly swallowed my tongue from the shock. Serena had never said a kind thing to me in all the years I'd known her. I inclined my head, not trusting myself to speak.

"She's a Familiar," my mother said, smoothly. "Of course she'd do what she could to save him."

Serena's lips tightened into a line so thin they nearly disappeared into her cadaverous face. "Very humorous, Katherine. Maybe if you had as much interest in doing your job as queen as you apparently have in trying to tweak me, the current mess wouldn't be happening."

I found her statement rich, considering the main reason Serena hated my mother was because she'd been chosen over the equally powerful high priestess to lead the magic-using community in the Human Realm.

Mother very graciously inclined her chin, her tone carefully modulated. "I'll accept my portion of the blame in this, Serena. But, as you know, I am no longer queen. We all serve equally on the council. Therefore, each of us shoulders a share of the blame. Don't you agree?" Her smile was so sweet I was pretty sure everybody in the room gained a pound just looking at it.

Serena glowered down her long, slightly hooked nose at my mother. I couldn't help wondering if she went out of her way to make herself look exactly like the human portrayal of the wicked witch, or if it just came naturally to her.

All she was missing was the nose wart, green-tinged skin, and pointy hat to complete the picture.

Eglund, King of the Trolls, scratched his bulbous nose with the side of a wide finger and frowned at Serena. "The infighting won't help us at all," he said in a voice that sounded like a rockslide on a mountain slope. He looked at me, a smile on his broad, craggy face as he reached for my hands. "Thank you for bringing my people safely back, young woman."

I thought about poor Deergart succumbing to my errant spell and then suffering a sword wound when I turned medieval on the *Axismundi* soldier's butt and flushed. "I did no more than anyone else, Your Highness. Your people were brave and strong in a difficult situation. They represented the Troll nation well."

It was the highest compliment I could give the Troll King and the wide smile splitting his face showed I'd hit the intended mark. "Thank you, child."

"Let's get started," Serena demanded in her high-pitched, nasally voice. "The sooner we fix this, the sooner we can get back to normal council business."

Part of which included planning the vote for a new queen, which was why she had her striped socks in a twist over getting back to it. Despite my mother's attempts to flatten out the ruling structure in the Human Realm, there were enough of the old guard still in place that she couldn't keep them from trying to return things to the way they'd been. The only thing my mother could do was hope she was selected again, so she could proclaim that she would rule as one of twelve equal members of the council.

Given enough time, her hope was that the others would grow accustomed to the idea.

Serena's well-known ambition was to make sure that didn't happen. She had designs on becoming the first high priestess who also carried the title of Queen of the Council. She wouldn't wear the crown well. Even her Witches knew that. Witches and Familiars were in staunch agreement. We'd all made it our unspoken objective to make sure Serena never got close enough to that virtual crown to even imagine its weight.

"Where's Trudy?" Mandy asked on a frown. "I didn't see her at the office."

Mother slid a look my way, holding my gaze as she answered. "She had some business in *Mundala*. She'll be here soon. Hopefully, she'll have information that will help."

I held her gaze, feeling my stomach churn with nerves. She knew. She'd read between the lines of what I'd told her and figured out what her sister had done.

It was the only thing that explained her mention of *Mundala*, which was the throne city in *Axismundi* and the seat of all power there. *Mundala* was the place where Trudy had once led the realm from her pretty treetop castle.

I turned to Tollman. "Tell them what you told us."

The Angel quickly explained about Anthrall taking the human form of Graham Cullpepper, as well as his speculation about the other Angel's purpose in the Human Realm.

He was interrupted a few times with questions. He answered them as quickly and informatively as he could.

By the time his last response died between us, everyone had grim expressions on their faces.

Finally, Eglund asked the question I'd expected much earlier in the meeting. "Why have you brought us here? Why are we not sitting in council as we should be?"

Mother looked to Tollman, her expression slightly pinched. I knew it must be difficult for her to accept that someone at *Familiar, Inc.* might be Anthrall's inside man... or gal. But I wasn't sure why it was difficult. We'd certainly had spies there before.

"In order for him to get so many Wraiths in place and create an entire support structure in The Guild..." Tollman began.

His words shocked me into interrupting. "Wait! You're saying Anthrall created the Sensitives?"

"Not their latent magical abilities, no. But I'm certain he used his knowledge of magic to help them enhance what little they were born with. And I also don't doubt he augmented them where necessary to give them confidence."

"How did that happen without you knowing what he was?" I asked Tollman angrily.

The Angel turned a neutral expression my way. "A masked Angel is nearly impossible to recognize. Even by someone from the Celestial Realm."

"How is that possible?" Mandy asked.

"Because every Angel was once human," he responded, his gaze staying on mine. "It is our natural state. Therefore, it isn't really a mask at all."

I held his stare for a moment and then nodded. What he said made sense.

"Okay, so Anthrall created his little group of magic

users," Mandy said. "Then it was just a matter of putting a bug in the Sensitives' ears about exposing the magic community so they could go public with their own abilities once the furor died down." She nodded. "He probably convinced them they'd be powerful and revered for their magic." She curled her lip. "How could he not know what that would do to the rest of us?"

"I'm sure he knew exactly what that would do," Mother said. "Wouldn't you agree, Mr. Tollman?"

"I'm afraid so." Tollman scrubbed a big hand over his chin, the ever-present bristles rasping against his palm. "Anthrall's been in an in-between place for centuries. He's been a king in his world but a pawn of the Celestial Court. He's become increasingly angry. And his anger is focused on two things: grabbing power for himself and controlling the most important realm to use against the court."

"What you're telling us is that we're stuck between a disgruntled Angel and an arrogant Celestial Court?" Mandy asked in her usual take-no-prisoners way.

"I'm afraid that's the nut of it," Tollman agreed.

"So how do we stop him?" Eglund asked.

"Our attack is going to have to be two-fold," Tollman responded. "Anthrall has a circle of Wraiths around him. As we recently learned, they're virtually indestructible."

"But we have a supply of those flowers," Brock said.

"Yes, they will succumb to the effects of the *dulcemori*. But the result won't be as potent here. The magic in the blooms is targeted toward the energy of the Tenth."

Silence pulsed between us. I swallowed hard as I realized our secret weapon might not be as powerful as we'd assumed. "They won't work here?"

Tollman scanned me a look, his navy gaze wary. "I didn't say that. But only the deadliest part of the plant will kill the Wraiths in this realm. The poison the flowers eject will barely slow the creatures down."

"You're talking about the cinnamon scented stuff?" I asked.

He nodded.

"Then, what *is* the deadliest part? Please don't say the roots because I didn't bring roots back with me." As I said the words, I realized how stupid I'd been. As an earth Familiar, gaining my power from plants and things that grow from the soil, I of all people should have realized the roots were vital. But we'd been under threat of the Wraiths finding us at any moment, and Brock and I had cut the stems as quickly as we could.

"The petals. Unfortunately, in order for the poison to work, the Wraiths will need to ingest them."

I bit back a groan. "We need to get our potion into that acid-filled slit in their bellies?"

"Yes."

"Ugh!"

"I think I have an idea for how to do that," Brock said.

Tollman glanced his way. "Good. We'll talk about that in a minute. In the meantime, we need to discuss Anthrall's...disposal." He grimaced as he said the word.

I recognized it couldn't be easy for him to talk about killing his friend. "Maybe it won't come to that," I offered weakly.

Tollman looked down at his hands on the table, his mouth twisting in a bitter smile. "I'm afraid that I'm the only one powerful enough to deal with him."

The room was silent for a long moment. Finally, my mother spoke up. "Can you do it?"

The meaning behind her question was clear. We all knew he *could* do it if he was committed to the act.

However, the fact that he'd already failed in that endeavor once, as well as his obvious misery at the idea of trying again, created reasonable doubt. I was pretty sure we were all wondering the same thing.

When push came to actual shove, would Tollman do whatever it took to stop his friend?

NINETEEN

"Mother?"

She halted at the door as she was about to leave with the other council members, turning back. "Yes?"

"Can you stay a minute longer, please? I need to talk to you about something."

She turned to Serena. "I'll see you back at the office."

The Witch slid her cold black gaze my way, her lips pinched, and then nodded.

I pulled air into my lungs as Mother closed the door behind the council and Tollman. In a way, I was looking forward to talking to Mother about my worries. But I was also dreading it. I was terrified she'd tell me exactly the opposite of what I wanted to hear.

"What's wrong, peaches?"

I twisted my fingers nervously in front of me, not sure how to begin. My mother hadn't exactly been a huge fan of my continued connection to Celeste after my grandmama had died. I'd chalked it up to jealousy at first. Celeste had always been my chosen confidante growing up. That hadn't changed when I'd become an adult. It had always rubbed my mother the wrong way.

But if I were honest with myself, I had to admit Mother probably didn't want me to get hurt. She wanted me to face the fact that Celeste had moved on.

She wanted me to move on too.

"Grandmama Celeste has gone incommunicado. I'm worried about her."

Mother frowned. "LeeAnn..."

I held up a hand. "Before you just dismiss it out of hand, Trudy spoke to her about the Wraiths before we left. Celeste was going to do some checking with the Celestial Realm on who might be driving them. I'm worried Anthrall found out and did something to her."

Mother pursed her lips and crossed her arms over her chest. Her gaze was filled with pique. I fought the urge to defend myself and waited. She'd either get over the fact that Celeste and I had been staying in touch, or she wouldn't. That was out of my control.

But when she finally spoke, it wasn't what I expected. "Trudy's been communicating with your grandmother too?"

Too late, I realized my mistake. "I...I'm sure it was just this once."

"Are you?" Her posture had gone rigid with anger. But it was the tears shimmering in her pretty gaze that tore my heart to bits. "Is there no end to your aunt's duplicity?" She scrubbed a hand over her eyes and sniffled.

I reached out and clasped her hand, giving it a squeeze. "Trudy loves you. She loves all of us." I wasn't a hundred percent sure that was true, but I'd felt the need to say it.

Mother sniffed again and sighed. "When was the last time you spoke to Celeste?"

"Well, as I said, Trudy spoke to her..."

Mother shook her head. "Not Trudy. You have only her word for it that she spoke to your grandmother at all. When did *you* last speak to her?"

With a jolt, I realized she was right. If Trudy had been lying to us all along, I had no reason to believe she wasn't lying about that too. "When the Wraiths attacked Deg and me." I frowned. "She helped, I think. I don't know how she did it, but she somehow shoved the thing, buying me some time. Then she told me how to kill it." I blinked. *I knew how to kill them*. But it had been terrifying and painful and dangerous. And I'd barely managed to take down one of them. If Anthrall had dozens, I couldn't possibly do what I'd done before. We needed to find an easier way.

I pulled myself out of my thoughts and looked at Mother. She was staring into space, her expression thoughtful.

"Mother?"

She jerked her gaze to me. "It's possible. But it takes vast amounts of energy. And no small amount of skill. I can't think of more than one or two people who could accomplish it. Your grandmother is one, of course." To my vast surprise, pride threaded her tone.

"*What's* possible?"

Mother started to pace the hallway, her hands moving in front of her as she spoke. She was excited. More excited than I'd ever seen her. "You know that power you have? Where you can reach into a person's soul and extract their final moments?"

I nodded. I'd been told all my life that it was a rare skill. That I was the only Familiar ever known to have inherited it. There were apparently a couple of Witches who could do it, but they were almost as rare. I'd never met one.

"This is a form of that. Rather than manipulating another's soul, it requires expanding your own soul, sending it across time and space. Celeste has played with it in the past, but she was never able to pull it off with much accuracy. She eventually gave it up."

"So, you think Celeste projected her soul at the Wraith?"

"Technically it would have been more like a punch. But accessing that kind of power would have been very draining. It could explain why you haven't heard from her. Entering the ether between the Fields and this realm takes its own level of energy. She might not have the reserves right now."

I grinned. "That makes sense."

She nodded, actually giving a happy little chuckle. "The old bird still has it."

We shared a laugh and it felt good. Her explanation had made me feel better. And that meant I could focus on the problem at hand. Then I had a thought. "Do you think I could learn to do that?"

Mother's eyes went wide. "Possibly. It would be a useful skill to have." She shook a finger at me. "Remind me to set you up with a trainer when this is behind us. I'd like to know if you're capable of that too."

I nodded. "Thanks."

She pulled me into an impulsive hug. "I'm glad Celeste was there when you needed her." She sounded sad. I wasn't sure if it was because she still missed her mother, or if she was sad because I'd called my grandmama instead of her in my moment of need. "Mother, you know why I asked for Celeste and not you, right?"

She nodded, scraping the heel of her hand under her eyes. "In all matters death and ether, she's definitely the expert."

I gave her a sad smile. "Unfortunately, yes."

"Okay," Mother said, returning to business. "We'll see you at the office? We need to work out the details of the plan. As soon as Tollman locates Anthrall, we need to move. I can't shake the feeling that we're working on borrowed time."

I nodded, watching her stride purposely toward the door. I agreed with her about the borrowed time thing. I could feel the other shoe hovering above our heads, ready to drop.

Anthrall was clearly not stupid. And he was ambitious enough to fight for what he wanted. I doubted he was going to just roll over and give up. He knew we were coming for him. And I had no doubt we were in for the fight of our lives in defeating him.

OSCAR MET me at the front entrance when I arrived, his face flushed and his eyes wide. "Hurry!" He turned on his heel and strode quickly toward the elevator.

"What's going on?" I had to run to catch up.

He ignored my question as the elevator door closed and then opened on the other side at the clinic level.

"Oscar? Tell me what's happening."

Stepping out in front of me, he jerked his head toward the glass doors. "They're waiting for you."

I gave up trying to get him to answer my questions and headed for the clinic, my mood decidedly foul. I was getting pretty sick of my mother's assistant. He was way too much about the drama for my taste.

My nerves were already on edge. Oscar's, *'you're late,*

you're late, for a very important date' demeanor had created a ball of acid in my belly that I really didn't need.

I shoved the door open and saw the group of people clustered together over in the seating area. Heads turned as I approached and I was met by several smiling faces. The group split apart, opening up a view to the two men who were seated on the couch. They looked much better than the last time I'd seen them.

My face split in a wide grin. "Deg!" I hurried over and wrapped my arms around him, hugging him tightly as I inhaled his wonderful scent. "You look great!"

Several cleared throats later, I let him go and turned to Littleton. Instead of the hug, I opted for taking one of his hands and squeezing it. "Thank goodness you're okay. I have a hankering for some frosted sugar cookies."

The Elf shook his head, chuckling. He still looked tired, his almost-too-handsome face lined and not completely back to a healthy shade, but he smiled and it reached his eyes. "No cookies just yet. But I feel better and I'm getting out of this terrible place soon."

Mandy frowned, and he held up a hand. "Nothing about the care I've received. You healers have worked miracles. But I'm ready to be home."

I could understand that sentiment.

"Besides," Brock said, dropping an arm over Mandy's shoulders. "The miracles are still coming."

Mandy flushed with embarrassment.

"What's happened? Did you come up with a way to kill the Wraiths?" I asked hopefully

"Not kill them, no," Mandy said, grinning widely.

I narrowed my gaze. "Okay."

Everyone around me chuckled. "Better, I think," said

Mandy. "We've figured out how to reverse the spiritual degradation."

"Huh?" I asked stupidly.

"Well, one of the other healers made the comment that the poison was acting like a virus. And I thought, well, that's stupid..." She turned to give a pretty, green-haired Witch a grin. I recognized her as the one who'd promised to keep Oscar at bay when I'd come to see Deg the first time. "Nothing personal, Jenny."

The other woman laughed gaily. "None taken."

"Of course, it's not a virus. But she was right. It *did* act like a virus. So, I examined that cinnamon stuff the flowers emitted and realized it had some of the markers of a super-virus. One that enhanced a disease which was already pretty far along. I wanted to find out why Tollman said the poison wouldn't kill the Wraiths here..."

"Could I maybe get the abbreviated version of this?"

Mandy gave me her special, *Sorry, I forgot you were stupid*, look. "We created a Wraith cure."

My mouth fell open. "You did what, now?"

She slammed her hands onto her narrow hips and glared at me. "LA, I don't know how I can make it any easier to understand."

I held up a hand. "No, I understand the statement, but I'm a bit baffled by the idea of a cure. Can people be cured of a bad soul? Because that's basically what those things are. They're the product of a lifetime and beyond of pure evil."

"Yes. And no. Well, maybe."

"Okay. That covers it."

Mandy shook her head. "What I mean is, we don't know if the cure will *fix* their souls. The key thing isn't whether they come out of this as good people. We don't care about that. The key is that they'll be people. Or at least not indestructible Wraiths."

I blinked at her.

She leaned closer, her expression impatient. "They'll. Be. People."

Then it hit me. "Mortal! Easy to kill...or capture."

"Yes!"

"Gargoyle whiskers!" I breathed. "That's amazing."

Mandy nodded, beaming with pride.

"Okay, so how do we administer this stuff?"

Her smile fell away.

Oh, oh.

"That's where it gets a bit tricky," Brock said.

"It needs to be injected behind their ears," Mother said.

"They have ears?" I asked. Clearly, the full impact of the statement hadn't hit me yet.

"They do," Jenny said, frowning. "But you have to get really close to see them."

"How close?" I asked, the full extent of the problem finally hitting me.

"Too close," Deg said. "We need to find another way."

I held his gaze for a moment and realized he was worried for my safety. And maybe just a little bitter that he wouldn't be in the fight.

"There is no other way, Deg," Mandy said in her snottiest voice. "Behind the ears, there's a vein that leads directly into their digestive systems. If we inject it there, it will work almost immediately. If we inject it anywhere else, it will take several minutes to work. We won't have several minutes once we attack."

I frowned. "How do you know that?"

She shrugged. "Brock found an old medical text from the Hades library in King Al's study."

I glanced at my friend and saw sadness flicker across his face. His people had recently lost King Alabast and had yet to replace him. It was a difficult time for Demons in the Human Realm. I suspected that was why my mother had been keeping him busy with Troll plumbing and such. To keep his mind off things.

I shook my head. "Let's think about this for a minute. Celeste told me when we fought the last batch of these things that controlling the leader Wraith controls all of them." I looked at Mandy. "Is that true?"

She shook her head. "I don't know. The text didn't talk about controlling them."

"We need to know for sure," Deg said.

"We aren't going to know for sure," I told him angrily. "Celeste is offline. I can't reach her. We're on our own. I think we need to go with the best information we have. If we can take down the leader, I'm ninety percent sure we'll be able to at least weaken them all. Then we can inject them."

"Ninety percent isn't sure enough with these things," Deg said. "What if the others are released from the lead Wraith's control once he's gone? There are too many components we don't understand."

"It's what we have, Deg," I countered.

"Assuming we agree to this," Serena said. "How will we control the leader long enough to inject the poison?"

"A holding spell?" Jenny asked.

"I don't think that will work on these things," a deep voice said from behind me. I turned to find Tollman strolling toward us.

Mother stepped forward. "You've found him?"

Tollman nodded, his expression unreadable.

"I can hold the lead Wraith," I told everyone.

"Absolutely not," Deg said, his concern turning to anger. "It's too dangerous."

"I can do it. I already did it once."

"When!" he demanded.

"When you were..." I stopped as I saw the color leech from his face. "At Guild headquarters. Celeste walked me through it."

"And you were nearly killed," Brock put in with a scowl. "I agree with Deg. It's too dangerous."

"It's the only option we have," I told them. I was determined not to let them win. I could control the Wraith for the few seconds it would take to inject it.

"It will take too long to inject the others," Mandy said.

When I glared at her, she shrugged. "Sorry, LA. I'm all for girl-power and I'm not doubting your abilities, but there could be fifty of these things for all we know. Injecting each one will take a few seconds or more. Their skin is very thick. We might break needles. Holding the leader off for that long will kill you. I'm not willing to risk that."

"We can remove that as a problem," King Eglund said.

Everyone turned to look at him. "We can inoculate them all in a matter of seconds."

"How?" Deg and Brock asked simultaneously.

King Eglund looked to Deergart, who I was happy to see was looking much better. "Have you briefed the archers?"

I frowned. "Archers?"

Eglund nodded. "It's well known that Trolls are good with our blades. But less well known that we're highly-skilled with a bow and arrow. We've selected the best of the best for this task."

"Genius!" Mandy said. "We'll tip the arrows with the potion."

I nodded. "Then, I only need to hold the lead long enough for one of your men to hit him with an arrow," I told Eglund.

"Not so fast," Tollman said. "How much of this potion is needed to kill the Wraiths?" he asked Mandy.

She didn't bother correcting him about the result. "A few drops. If we paint the entire tip of the arrow, it should be enough."

"Then the lead Wraith will need double that amount. Maybe triple."

I barely bit back a groan.

Tollman gave me an apologetic smile. "He'll have been in the Tenth for millennia. It's the only way he'd have enough power to hold so many Wraiths enthralled."

"He'll need to be injected," Deg said. He stood up, the color flooding from his face as he gripped the arm of the couch. "I'll inject the leader while LA holds it."

I was already shaking my head, but he glared back at me. "I can tell I'm not going to be able to talk you out of this, so I'm going to help. End of discussion."

Tollman stopped my argument before it got started. "Okay, let's go then. I don't want Anthrall to move again before we have a chance to surround him."

TWENTY

Fog drifted around us, swirling lazily at my feet. I squinted through the dense soup, unable to see five feet away. The mist had an icy quality to it that chilled me deep down into my bones and left me feeling wet and sloggy.

The warm front that had moved in to create the fog had melted the snow on the ground, leaving behind ice-dotted puddles and mud the consistency of gargoyle snot.

My feet were frozen inside my soggy boots. My fingers felt like they might fall off, despite the leather gloves covering them.

I shivered violently and jumped as a tall form emerged from the fog.

Deg still looked too pale, his gaze slightly feverish, but he seemed stronger since eating and making himself an energy potion. "It's quiet. Too quiet. Tollman's starting to wonder if Anthrall moved on."

"The Wraiths are here," I told my Witch.

He looked a question at me, and I shrugged.

I didn't know if Anthrall had moved on, but his Wraiths

were still there, somewhere in the cloaking fog. I didn't know how I knew they were there. I just did.

It was as if I could feel their magic trembling in the air.

"Where's Tollman?" I asked Deg.

He pointed toward the hazy wall of white. "Out there. Somewhere." He frowned. "This fog is killing us. How are we supposed to coordinate anything, let alone have archers hit their mark with this kind of visibility?"

I didn't know the answer to that. I only knew we didn't have a choice.

The murk shifted again, and Mandy strolled out of it. She looked at Deg. "We need to do something with this mist."

He nodded. "I was thinking the same thing. A purifying spell?"

"I considered that, but there's no guarantee it would give us the kind of purity we need. I was thinking a straining spell."

He thought about it for a minute. "Nothing to strain here. Unless you think the fog is a spell."

They started to talk spells and magic signatures and other boring stuff. I decided to let them do their thing without me. "I'm going to find Tollman."

I left them arguing quietly about which spell they were going to use and plunged into the smog. As I walked blindly through it, I thought back to another time Deg and I had fought through smoggy air with low visibility in that very same place. The old Guild headquarters had been burning then. The fog had been a thick, light-gray smoke, and it had sucked all the oxygen out of the air at the time.

The current smog smelled better. Though the things waiting for us inside the fog were much deadlier than they'd been last time.

I walked for several minutes without finding Tollman or anyone else. I longed to call out to him, but knew it might bring the wrong kind of response heading my way. Instead, I pressed my lips together and kept trudging through.

A prickle touched me through the fog. A whisper of energy that tasted like Deg's and Mandy's magic. They'd apparently decided on a spell.

Good. The sooner they could find a cure for the miasma, the sooner we could defeat the Wraiths and Anthrall and the sooner I could get home to a really hot, ridiculously long shower.

The magic slipped over me, comforting and warm, and the small hairs on my neck stood up in response.

A graveyard stench wafted past. I skidded to a halt.

Come.

I blinked. "Who's there?"

Come!

The voice was filled with a little more power the second time. I jolted forward, realizing with surprise and fear that I was being compelled.

I yanked my power forward and slipped it around me like a cloak. The voice remained quiet for a long moment, so I started forward again.

Anthrall was apparently up to no good. I didn't plan to get caught up in his Wraith trap.

The fog drifted around me, its icy tentacles climbing down the neckline of my coat and turning the skin of my face to ice.

My toes ached from the cold, and my hair hung in icy strings down my back.

Mandy's and Deg's magic was a whisper outside my power coating, but I could see the results in the gradual thinning of the soup surrounding me.

Nice work, I told Deg in my mind.

He didn't respond. I figured he was too busy weaving magic. A rhythmic *thump, thump, thump* sounded overhead. I glanced up and saw the enormous, black shape of Brock's demonic form high above me. He'd probably gone aloft to get out of the icy soup.

Smart. And had the added benefit of shoving some of the stuff away from me as he passed.

I stopped as the fog finally melted away. My gaze slid through the darkness, which seemed too opaque for the evening hour—even in the winter.

The burned-out husk of the old house where The Guild had shared a headquarters loomed high above my head. I realized I was standing in the driveway, much closer to the house than I would have guessed.

If Mandy and Deg hadn't gotten rid of the fog when they did, I might have run right into it.

The sour stench of wet, burned wood filled my nostrils as the fog left. As if the mist had been holding the smell in check.

I blinked. What if it had? That would mean...

Come!

I jerked, spun sideways, and started walking before my mind even registered what had happened.

It wasn't possible.

I tried to pull more energy into my protective magic, but it wouldn't come. In fact, I could no longer feel the energy cloak.

It had slipped away.

What was going on? Had the fog somehow taken my powers with it? No, that was crazy. Unless...

The concrete face of the passageway through which Deg and I had escaped the burning home came into view. It was pitch black inside that passage, even darker than the night beyond the entrance. I heard no sign that my friends were anywhere close.

Surely, they hadn't all left me behind? The thought dragged icy fingers of fear and rage out of hiding, and I growled, long and low in my throat. Claws sprang from my fingertips as I lost control of my feline form.

My skin itched and then tingled. Fur sprang from my pores. I'd fallen to my knees and my back was bowing under my change before I realized I was no longer alone in the dark.

Orange, flickering light flared into the blackness not more than ten feet away.

Eyes.

I'd seen those eyes before. Paler orange and red flares appeared on either side of the lead Wraith, steady and bright against their shadowy forms.

The graveyard stench I'd smelled before thickened the air, putrid and horrible. It was stronger with the mist gone. Or maybe it was because I was using my feline senses. Looking down, I realized I'd only partly shifted.

Impossible.

Biting back panic, I concentrated on shoving my shifting magic back into the place where it belonged and felt it slowly ease away. A moment later, panting from the effort and achy from the near shift, I straightened and stood.

Come!

I tried to deny the command. But as the lead Wraith turned and headed into that terrifyingly dark passage, my feet started to move and, Heaven help me, I began to follow.

Deg!

The other Wraiths fell in around me, their stench making my eyes water and my steps falter. I fought the compulsion with everything I had but realized I was going to have to get creative to beat it.

The moment we stepped into the big house, ancient warding magic made it impossible for me to use my powers.

I swiveled my head as I walked, looking for anything I could use to escape the Wraiths. I had no idea why they were bringing me into the burned-out headquarters, but I knew whatever the reason, it wasn't going to end well for me.

Or for my friends.

A moment later I saw the slashes and swirls of the binding magic scrawled over the moist rock of the passage walls. Deg and I had identified the spell when we'd come through the tunnel before.

I didn't recognize any of the symbols. They'd been created well before my time. But I knew that one thing probably hadn't changed over the centuries. At least I was counting on it not having changed. Because if I couldn't find a way to interrupt the warding's effectiveness, my friends and I had no chance in the coming battle.

My feet plodded forward. I watched in a panic as the inscription on the wall passed on by. There were two rows of symbols, the entire thing encompassing a space about eight feet by three feet. The characters were written in very large swirls and slashes, each symbol no less than twelve inches tall. I didn't know if that was to give them more power, or because the tool used to inscribe them couldn't be adapted to finer writing.

It didn't matter. For my purposes it was good that the spell took up such a large space on the wall. It gave me more time.

I gritted my teeth and focused on stopping my forward motion. The best I could manage was to slow it. My feet tried to tug away from my control, and I stumbled as I wrested temporary control. My left foot shot sideways as a result. I fell against the cold, slimy wall, my hand slapping against the very bottom of the second row of figures.

I had only a second to do what needed to be done.

I had no time to consider my options.

My rogue shifting energy seemed the likeliest option in a list of very limited choices.

As in a list of one.

With a growl of fury and effort, I grabbed my cat and ripped it out of its hidey hole at my core, embracing the burning pain of a violent, too-rapid shift. As soon as the claws slipped from my fingertips, I threw my arm up and slashed downward, tearing chunks of wet rock away with the razor-sharp claws.

I broke the spell by breaking the symbols.

The effect was immediate. The Wraiths threw back their misshapen heads and shrieked. The force of their screams was unbearable. It tore into my head, ripping at my eardrums and making my brain feel like mush. I dropped to my knees and covered my ears, tears of blood running down my cheeks and falling onto my soggy jeans.

My screams joined theirs. The Wraith's cries tore at me like blades, growing in intensity by the second, and I folded into a fetal position on the frosty ground in an attempt to escape them.

Something popped inside my head. Something tore. Warm moisture ran from every orifice in my head and I went limp.

The shrieking stopped, but the damage was already done. I couldn't move. Couldn't form a single thought. No longer knew where I was. No longer cared.

I was vaguely aware of being lifted roughly off the ground and carried through darkness into flickering light.

Warmth found me. Heat so delicious it dispelled the debilitating cold almost immediately. I was flung onto the floor. My bones were jolted by the landing, but it wasn't as painful as it should have been.

Light flared and danced around me, painting my immobile form with warm colors. Wood smoke filled the room. It wasn't sour like what I'd smelled outside. It was sweet and comforting.

A rhythmic sound came to me. *Click, click, click.* I tried to lift my head to see what it was, but I couldn't move.

Voices erupted into the silence. One shrill and one deep, melodic. A constant ringing in my ears made identifying the voices impossible. But if I concentrated, I could make out some of what they said.

"What were you thinking, bringing her here?"

"I was thinking...why not?" Humor threaded the deeper voice, and I found myself wanting to see who it belonged to.

"They'll come looking for her, you fool!"

"That's the idea, isn't it? Tollman thinks he can take me on. Let's see how much help he gets when her friends see what I've done to her."

Oh-oh. A strand of *maybe I do care* shivered through my mind. With that thought, my thoughts started to clear. I kept my eyes closed but pulled a slim thread of energy forward to heal the worst of my injuries.

"Just kill her, then, and be done with it. Or let me do it."

Light flashed, visible through my lids, and shrill-voice yelped. "Do not presume too much!" the deeper voice boomed. "You will gain much from my work here. But you will still work for me. Do you understand?"

A murmured response sifted past, too soft for me to hear.

"What?" the deep voice boomed.

"I said, yes. I understand."

"Good. Now go. Before the others come."

I felt the brush of something move past and fought the urge to look up. I assumed the owner of the deeper voice was Anthrall.

It appeared that the owner of the shrill voice knew my friends. I thought of Tollman's fear that Anthrall had a spy at *Familiar, Inc.* The one with the shrieky intonation had to be that person. But I hadn't been able to identify the voice.

String her up, the deep voice said inside my mind. He was obviously talking to the Wraiths, but I recognized the voice from before. It had been Anthrall himself who'd summoned me there. But how could he have that kind of influence over me? Was he really that powerful?

Hard hands grabbed my arms and legs, lifting me into the air. That was the moment I realized it was time to stop playing dead. If I didn't do something soon, I wouldn't have to *play* at being dead because I'd *be* dead.

And worse, Anthrall would use my death against my friends.

I yanked my power from its core and opened my eyes. Without giving myself time to reconsider it, I pierced the two Wraiths holding me aloft with my tracking energy, the energy surging toward the twisted remains of their wretched souls and wrapping around the husks. I amped up, turning the husks to ash and slashing upward with my energy to sever the monsters' heads from their bodies.

I landed on my feet as they dropped me and sent my energy into another two Wraiths. I'd burned their souls to dust before something slammed into me, sending me flying across the room. I hit the wall so hard it knocked the air from my lungs. I landed on my knees, pain knifing up my legs from the impact, and fought to drag air into my chest.

"Nice try, Familiar. I'll admit I didn't think you had it in you." Anthrall glanced at his pets. "Go take care of the rest of them."

The Wraiths slipped silently away, leaving behind a residual stench that made me want to breathe through my mouth.

My head came up and I struggled to rise. Horrible sounds emerged from my chest as I fought to draw a breath.

Anthrall threw out a hand and I slammed backward again, smacking my skull hard against the wall. "I don't think so. I don't trust you at all."

Nausea roiled in my belly. Stars burst. My body wobbled from the dual torture of trying to breathe and having my brains scrambled again. I swallowed bile and looked up at him, fixing as much hatred onto my face as I could manage.

The creature standing a few feet away from me was huge. Probably closer to eight feet than Tollman's seven. He was perfection in a humanoid form.

Thick white-blond hair framed a chiseled face with a square jaw and piercing Caribbean blue eyes. I saw only the barest suggestion of Graham Culpepper in his looks. Unlike Tollman, Anthrall had used more artifice in his human form. The closest he came to any of Culpepper's traits was the rosebud mouth, which was slightly too small for his face and allowed me to visualize the anus lips of his alter ego.

When I'd drawn air and could finally speak, I tilted my chin up in feigned defiance and cracked wise in the hopes he'd be intimidated by my pluck.

"I like what you've done with the place, Anthrall.

Though I'd have thought you were more of a Mid-Century Modern kind of guy. This has a post zombie apocalypse feel to it that doesn't suit you."

He stared at me, unreactive.

Dang. That was some of my best stuff too.

"I like you, Ms. Mapes. It's really too bad I have to kill you."

"You don't really have to kill me. You have options."

He peaked his eyebrows. "I do? What are they, then?"

I shrugged, not wanting to go through his options, which wouldn't take very long and would leave me facing option number one. In other words, I'd be right back where I started. "My friends are going to end you no matter what you do to me. You might want to consider making a run for it."

He laughed. The sound turned my blood to sludge. It was filled with power that vibrated the walls and snuffed the flames out in the oversized fireplace.

"Tollman's a washed-up has-been. He has no idea what he's about to go up against."

"Why don't you tell me?" I prayed my friends had dispatched the Wraiths and were coming to help me soon. I was pretty sure the creature I was facing off with could extinguish me without even breaking a sweat.

"He doesn't know how much power I've absorbed on the Tenth. And the resistance I've gained there. I'm pretty much invincible now. Whereas he's...not."

"He's not alone," I reminded Anthrall.

"He will be. I can hear the screams of your people now. It won't be long before Tollman stands alone. He's hiding behind your friends, you know. Using them as shields. It's pathetic, really."

I blinked rapidly to keep the tears burning my eyes from

falling. Anthrall was lying. He had to be. My people weren't so easily dispatched. And Tollman...

Well, I really hoped Anthrall was lying about his friend. Because if he wasn't, I was going to have to kill two Angels for the price of one.

TWENTY-ONE

I pulled air into my lungs and dragged my power from the spot where it was cringing deep inside my body. I'd have to move fast, and I probably wouldn't get a second chance, so I needed to be accurate.

I knew as I closed my eyes and said his name there was a good chance he wouldn't respond.

I really needed him to respond.

Deg?

The silence in my head was like a thump to the gut, nearly buckling my knees.

Deg, I could use your help.

Static erupted in my brain, making me wince. His voice finally came to me, weak and thready through the noise. *LA? ...alright?*

I would have liked to ask him how it was going. But time was a luxury neither of us had. I didn't even have time to indulge in relief that he was still alive. *I need everything you've got.* And then some, I thought. *And I need Tollman in here. Now!*

More static. Deg didn't respond. I prayed he'd understood me.

And that he was all right.

"So quiet, LA. Does that mean you realize you've lost?"

I slowly pushed to my feet, taking my time and adding a little shakiness for effect. I pressed a hand against the wall as if I was having trouble standing. "All my friends are... dead?" I asked him in a soft voice filled with real fear.

He narrowed his gaze, cocking his head as he studied me. "Yes."

"What will you do with me?" I hadn't intended it, but the question came out wobbly with dread.

"That depends on you." His tone had changed too. He sounded confident, but he'd gentled his voice in an attempt to reel me in. "I could use your particular expertise if you want to join me."

"In what, exactly?" As I talked, I moved slowly forward, limping slightly for effect. Deg hadn't fed me any energy, and that told me everything I didn't want to know. It also firmed my resolve. If the monster standing across the room had killed my friends, he wasn't going to know what hit him. He'd likely kill me in the end. But I'd make sure he felt my rage before he did.

My skin crawled and my heart stuttered. I stopped as something moved just behind me. I jerked my head around, power flaring in my fingertips.

There was nothing there. I was seeing things. The slam against the wall must have done more damage to my head than I realized.

When I turned back to Anthrall, he wore a knowing smile. "You look ready for a fight, after all, Ms. Mapes."

I mentally scolded myself. I'd shown my hand too soon.

Oh well, might as well get it over with. I had an Angel to annoy.

I was suddenly flying across the room, with no clear memory of engaging the leap. I hit Anthrall hard, my nails sinking into his chest as my energy burst away from me in a bright, burning wash.

Anthrall stumbled back, surprise lighting his features for just a beat, but then the smug smile returned and he wrapped his hands around my shoulders, flinging me away.

I sailed backward and stopped, hanging in midair.

I wasn't sure which of us was more surprised, Anthrall or me. I'd never had the ability to fly or hover before. My mind replayed the attack on the soldier in Axismundi, the one attacking Deergart, and I realized I'd moved so quickly then I'd been nearly flying.

What had happened to me in *Underworld?* What had changed?

Anthrall glanced down at the bloody holes in his shirt. "Impressive. I underestimated you, LA." His gaze narrowed. "I won't do it again."

His hands lashed out, and I felt the impact of his power between my breasts. It didn't shove me away as I'd expected. Instead, it tugged on me, dragging me closer.

I fought him with everything I had, using every ounce of energy in my core, and managed to slow the impetus of his pull.

Something ripped inside me, searing pain tore through my limbs and sliced into my belly. All the air left my lungs and I flew in his direction, no longer able to resist.

I slammed to a stop mere inches away, my eyes level with his and my feet dangling above the floor.

He squeezed his hands closed. My heart compressed

painfully, feeling as if it would explode from the pressure he was exerting on it.

In sheer desperation, I gathered my tracking energy and threw it at him, slicing into his physical form and heading for the core of his power. Where he kept his soul form.

I recognized the energy immediately. It was the snippet of angelic energy I'd encountered before.

In Malice Becksmart's body.

My energy surrounded his, and tore into it, not bothering with finesse as my organs began to falter under his attack.

Anthrall's smug smile widened. "You think you can attack me as if I were a mere mortal?"

I didn't think that at all. But I had to try anything I could. I sent the last reserves of my energy into the magic I'd inserted into him and twisted it with my mind, creating a lethal corkscrew of power that sheered into him, tearing a finger sized hole through his core and flinging smoggy Celestial power away in fractured pieces that I knew would take some time to repair.

I felt his reaction in the tightening of pressure in my own chest. He was feeling the pain and reacting with more violence.

Gritting my teeth against the pain and weakness, I held on, determined to do as much damage as possible. If I could weaken him, Tollman and my friends could hopefully finish him off.

"Release me!"

The command slipped through my defenses and claimed my will, causing me to immediately retract my magic.

My eyes widening, I looked down at my hand and saw the charcoal gray magic slide out of him and back into my fingers, leaving behind a smoky aura that coated my entire arm.

What the...?

To my great dismay, I no longer had the will or the energy to attack him.

Anthrall flicked his fingers and I slammed backward, hitting the wall hard enough that I heard something in my back break.

Anguish spread across my torso. It suddenly hurt to breath. I slumped downward. I didn't have even enough power to heal myself.

The door across the room slammed open, and footsteps hurried into the room. Relief filled me. Someone had survived the Wraiths. If only I had enough energy to lift my head and see who it was.

"LA?"

I closed my eyes, saying a prayer of thanks. Deg was alive.

Magic infused me, bright and hot and oh so rejuvenating. My head shot up. My gaze met his.

He was staring at me as if I'd grown two heads. I pushed to my feet. "Deg, thank heavens. Where's Tollman?"

He continued to stare at me, his face filled with...fear.

"Deg? What's wrong?"

"You'll have to forgive him," Anthrall drawled smugly. "He's never seen your Wraith form, my dear. It's disconcerting."

My Wraith...? I looked down and gasped. The smoky aura I'd seen before hadn't vanished. It had grown and swelled, covering my entire body. Horror took the starch from my limbs, and I stumbled backward.

LA? Deg's voice in my head was so broken it drew my gaze to his. *What's happened to you?*

Kill him, Anthrall said in my mind. *Kill him now*.

To my horror, my body jerked forward, my feet moving swiftly toward Deg. I fought against it, even drawing on the energy given to me by Deg, but the compulsion of his voice was too strong. Before I could stop myself, I'd drawn enough energy into my hands to kill my friend. "Run!" I screamed at Deg. "Get Tollman!"

Deg threw himself sideways as I flung the killing force in his direction. Thankfully, the energy veered away at the last second and scorched a long trail across the wall instead of hitting him.

Deg rolled nimbly to his feet and lifted his hands, writing a spell upon the air. His fingers moved so rapidly my eyes couldn't follow them. I prayed he had something powerful in the works, because things were going from bad to much much worse fast.

The energy built again, burning my veins with its massive power. Against my will, my hands lifted, and my fingers straightened. I sighted Deg along my outstretched hands, the energy boiling toward release. With a growl of superhuman effort, I swung my hands away from Deg at the last moment and shot the magic into Anthrall.

I caught him off guard and he shot backward, slamming into the wall.

Light burst through the room. Blinding, white light that made it impossible to keep my eyes open. I screamed as the light burned against my skin and stumbled away, shielding my eyes behind an arm.

At first, I thought the light came from Anthrall. But the sound of crashing and bodies flying around the room told me Tollman had finally arrived.

I tried to stand, but my legs wouldn't work. I'd channeled too much energy in too short a time, and I was beyond exhausted.

And I'd tried to kill my partner. My best friend. I'd been infected by something horrific, and I wasn't safe to be around.

With a jolt, I realized I was a danger to my friends and family. I had to get away. With that thought, I shoved to my feet and, using the last dregs of my control, stumbled toward the torn spot in the wall that led to the passages.

LeeAnn!

I ignored Deg's voice in my head. He'd feel guilty for fearing me. He might even pretend he didn't care about the Wraith inside me. But I knew I couldn't risk being around him. Not when some powerful Angel could compel me to kill him.

I was vaguely aware of the battle I left behind. I said a silent prayer that Tollman would win. And I was thankful Deg was safe. I had reason to hope the others were safe too. I'd go away. I'd keep them safe from me.

And I wouldn't come back until I'd rid myself of the stain I'd gained in Axismundi.

With that thought, I staggered out into the icy night and turned away from the sound of voices and the lights flashing across the grounds from cars coming and going.

It looked like the battle was over outside. My friends had won.

That would have made me smile if my world hadn't just ended. I stumbled over a chunk of ice and nearly fell. Throwing my hands out, I caught myself before face-planting and shoved upright again.

As I lifted my head, something snapped on the air. A bright string of light cracked across the night in front of me and wrapped around my ribs, locking my arms to my sides.

The magic yanked me to a halt and I fell, my face hitting the icy ground with a painful crunch. I flailed against the restraint, growling and lashing out with the claws that shot from my fingertips as I fought my invisible foe.

"Watch the claws!" someone shouted.

Wings throbbed above my head. A dark form descended to the ground in front of me, big hands reaching out to pull me gently from the ground and cradle me against a broad chest. "Calm down, LA," Brock said, his deep voice rumbling through my body.

A slender shape marched toward me through the dark, her distinctive form backlit by the lights of the cars beyond. Mandy knelt beside me, giving me a long-suffering look as I thrashed and growled, impotent against the invasion inside me.

"You've made quite a mess of yourself, haven't you, cat?" She lifted a syringe between us and eyed it as she squirted a drop from its tip. "This will take care of things. You'll sleep. Tomorrow we'll sort through everything else."

I shook my head, shoving my Wraith downward as a sense of urgency forced my own personality to return. "Don't trust me, Mandy. He compelled me. I can't control…"

The needle pinched the flesh of my upper arm.

Tears slipped from my gaze. "Lock me up…" I said to her, my voice already fading. "Lock me…"

And the world slipped away.

TWENTY-TWO

"LA?"

The voice tugged at me, dragging me gently from sleep.

"Wake up, lazy bones."

I fought its pull, knowing somewhere in my mind that there was a reason I didn't want to wake up.

"Come on, you've slept long enough." A soft hand slapped at my cheek. Gently at first and then a little harder. "Wake up, cat!"

Mandy's snotty voice was like claws on a blackboard, ripping the last vestiges of sleep from my body. I cranked my eyes open and looked up at her, my mind muzzy. "Where am I?"

"Quiet." She placed her hand on my chest. A warm light slipped through my skin, prickly and invasive.

She withdrew the sensing magic a moment later. "All good." She actually smiled down at me, and I flinched.

"Has the world ended? Why are you being so nice?"

She rolled her eyes, standing. "You're not going to ruin my mood."

I shoved myself upright in the bed and went still, looking at my wrists. "I'm not chained."

She shook her head, disgust curling her lips. "Of course you're not chained."

"But I'm dangerous!" I pushed the covers back and started to climb out of bed. A wave of dizziness made me almost fall on my face.

Mandy grabbed my shoulders and shoved me back, covering me with the blankets again. "You're fine. I took care of that little infection you had."

My eyes went wide. "You did?" I ruthlessly squashed the flare of hope, instead narrowing my gaze on her. "How?"

She grinned. "You'll see. Later."

I didn't like that at all. "No, this is pretty important. I want to see right now."

She heaved out a disgusted sigh. "All right, I'll tell you. You're not in any shape to go to the prison clinic to see with your own eyes."

"Prison clinic? Do we have one of those?"

Amazingly, her grin widened. "We do now."

"Okay," I said, rubbing my forehead. "You're giving me a headache. I feel like I've fallen down the rabbit hole into opposite world..."

"Mixed metaphor, much?"

"Alliteration always?"

She laughed gaily, making the throbbing spot in my head pulse harder. "First, the highlights. Tollman kicked Anthrall's butt. He's been shipped back to the Celestial Realm for trial and hopefully a few millennia in the fiery pits."

"I'm not sure he'd..."

"The Wraiths are gone," she said, mowing right over me.

I held up a hand. "Explain *gone*."

"Gone. Poof. Kaput," she said, flinging her hands dramatically upward.

"Dead?"

"No. They're alive." She beamed down at me.

The tiny throbbing spot in my brain became a hammer. "You're happy that they're alive?"

"Yes!" Mandy clapped her hands.

"Freakin' frog warts, my head's going to explode."

The door to my room opened, and Brock came inside. He arched a brow when he saw me. "You look better. I have to admit I really didn't enjoy all that growling and spitting. It was too much like Thanksgiving dinner with my relatives."

I glared at him. "None of this is funny, you guys."

To my horror, they both burst into laughter. "You've lost your freaking minds. Where's the portal? I want to go back to the real world. I don't like it here."

Mandy's smile fell away and her habitual scowl returned. "Better?"

"Infinitely. Now explain what you mean about the Wraiths. Did you capture them?"

"Yes. They're in the prison clinic," Brock said. He reached over and plucked a bowl of something red and jiggly off my bedside table and started eating it.

Mandy slapped his hand. "That's for LA."

Grimacing at the jiggly stuff, I shook my head. "He's welcome to it."

Mandy huffed. "Okay, so you remember I'd created a potion to make the Wraiths vulnerable by returning them to humanoid form?"

I nodded and then regretted it as pain slammed through my skull.

"Well, it worked even better than I'd hoped. We knew we had to adjust it for this realm. I condensed the pulp from the flowers and added that poison Tollman said wouldn't work on them here. Then I added some of Deg and Littleton's blood…"

"Wait!" I threw up a hand. "Blood magic?"

"Well, duh, LA. These were creatures from Hell. Did you think I'd just sweeten it with fruit juice?"

Brock snickered, settling the empty bowl back onto the table. "It was ingenious really."

They shared a smile that made me feel a little bit like a third wheel. "What was ingenious?" I asked to draw their attention back to their story.

"The blood." Mandy clarified. "It had antibodies for the Wraith toxin."

I waited for her to tell me what that meant. When she didn't, I said, "And?"

"And it killed the Wraith poison in their souls. It returned their souls to normal. They're walking, talking, functioning humans again."

I looked from her to Brock, my mouth falling open as the meaning of what she was telling me hit home. "Seriously? They're purged of evil?"

She shrugged. "Not exactly. But they're alive. My potion worked. We're calling them *Immortuos*. We're not sure what they are exactly but they seem a lot less dangerous now. I'm hopeful that with some work we can return them to *Underworld*."

I thought about what she'd said. If she'd found a way to kill the Wraith poison, did that mean she'd killed mine too? There was only one way to find out. I asked her the question.

She nodded. "We've seen no sign of it returning. I've

had the best healers we have in here, testing, observing. We've treated you three times just to be sure. You're clean."

Relief filled me and I finally relaxed. "I have no words." Tears filled my eyes.

Mandy flipped her hand dismissively. "All in a day's work."

I laughed. "Right. I'm pretty sure nobody will ever talk to me again after what happened."

I caught her and Brock sharing a look and frowned. "What aren't you telling me?"

They glanced at each other again. A guilty look passed between them.

"What? You're scaring me."

Mandy sighed. "We treated ourselves too. Just in case."

"The Wraiths got to you out there?"

"Not in the battle, no," Brock said. He moved closer, lowering his voice. "But we think we're responsible for their being here."

I started to argue and then stopped, thinking back to the trip to *Axismundi* when I'd thought I'd lost them both. And their subsequent insistence that something shadowy had fled them as they woke up in the Human Realm. Nobody had known how they'd gotten back. "You must have crossed into the Tenth," I breathed.

Mandy frowned, nodding. "It's the only thing we can think of. I'm guessing Anthrall had something to do with that."

She was right. He'd been looking for souls to corrupt. Brock and Mandy had no doubt seemed like the perfect vehicles for his pets. "Ugh."

"Yeah. That's pretty much how we feel too," Mandy said. "So, you see, we understand what you went through. We've even wondered at times if the infection stayed with us beyond what we thought. We'll never know. But now at least we can take comfort in the knowledge that the stain has been scoured away."

I nodded then fell back against the pillows. "I'm really tired."

Mandy patted my hand. "Sleep. You'll have more visitors later, I'm sure. As soon as everybody finds out you're awake."

I doubted that. Not after I'd attacked Deg. And after they learned I'd been a Wraith. But I didn't say anything. Given what I'd just learned about my friends' own Wraith experience, I didn't want to make them feel bad.

I dozed for a while, nasty dreams waking me up so many times it was almost a relief when a knock sounded on my door. I opened my eyes and called out, "Come in." My chest tightened with fear and hope that it would be Deg.

It wasn't.

Mother walked over and leaned down, placing a kiss on my forehead. "How are you feeling, peaches?"

"Tired but good."

She nodded, glancing around the room. "Mandy told you what happened?"

I nodded.

She squeezed my hand. "Everyone's very proud of you, LeeAnn. I'm very proud of you."

"Why?"

"Why? Because you did what was necessary at great risk to yourself. Because you saved us all from those monsters. You brought back those flowers, and you faced Anthrall alone."

"I really had no choice. And I almost killed Deg."

She frowned. "But you didn't, LeeAnn. You fought the

compulsion. That took a lot of grit. You're more powerful than you give yourself credit for."

I shrugged. "Is he mad at me?" It seemed such a silly question. But it was the most important thing in that moment.

"Deg? No. He's not mad."

But he was *something*. I could hear it in her voice.

"Then why isn't he here?"

"He'll come. He's just very busy right now."

"Busy? Nice euphemism."

She looked astonished. "Your friends didn't tell you?"

"Tell me what?"

"Deg's preparing to become the high priest of the coven."

All the blood left my face. "He's marrying Serena?" My voice had a dreadful screeching quality that made my mother wince. "No, of course not. Child, you really need to study up on Witch culture. Serena's been removed from her position on the council and as the leader of the Witches. She'll be tried in the Court of Magic soon for high treason. Deg is succeeding her."

I stared blankly at her for a moment, and then it all fell into place. "Of course! The fog."

"Yes. Deg recognized her signature in the magic that created it. She'd tried to interfere with our plan. To make it impossible to take out the Wraiths. But she hadn't counted on her own Witches being able to overwhelm her spell."

Shrill voice! How could I not have known it was her? "What a witch with a B."

Mother laughed. "Yes. Exactly. She was willing to throw us all over just so she could become Queen of the Council." She stood up and headed for the door. "As soon as you're up to it, come and see me. We'll talk about your role in the new hierarchy.

I was so stunned I didn't speak. I watched her leave, a feeling of unease sliding through me. My new role? What exactly did that mean? I wasn't sure I wanted to find out.

My life always seemed to be changing. And the changes never made things less complicated.

LeeAnn!

I jumped as my grandmama's voice filled my head. *Celeste. I've been so worried about you!*

There's no time for niceties now, child. Trudy's in terrible trouble. You need to come to Mundala as soon as possible.

Mundala? Are you crazy? She stabbed us in the back again. I'm washing my hands of her.

No, you are not, LeeAnn Mapes! Trudy has done what needed to be done. She did it for you and your mother. And now you need to do what's necessary to help her. Now get off your lazy bottom and get back here. She hasn't got much time.

I groaned loudly. *Celeste? Grandmama?* Just perfect! She was gone again.

As I was saying. Things *never* seemed to get *less* complicated. And it appeared I was off on another adventure.

The End

READ MORE RELUCTANT FAMILIAR BOOKS

I hope you enjoyed **Nothing Familiar**. Have you read the other books in the series?

Book 1: Familiar Territory
Book 2: A Familiar Problem
Book 3: Familiar Hijinks
Book 4: Nothing Familiar

Check out the entire series here: https://samcheever.com/books/#Reluctant

Please enjoy Chapter One, **Book 1: Familiar Territory** as my gift to you.

Familiar Territory

Independence is the most important thing to LA…but can she live with herself if her freedom ends up costing her family their lives?

She'd watched a friend succumb to the smothering control of another magical user. She'd made a promise to herself it would never happen to her. For centuries her family has worn the badge of Familiar proudly, serving a long line of powerful Witches and becoming as formidable as the ones they served. But LA doesn't believe she needs a Familiar alliance to be strong.

Until people she cares about begin disappearing... turning up dead.

Until a powerful and handsome male Witch walks into her life and forges an inadvertent magic bond while trying to save her life.

Now she finds herself in exactly the position she never wanted. But she quickly realizes she can't save her friends and family alone. So it comes down to losing her independence or watching everyone she cares about die.

Will LA find a way to keep her independence and still save the people she cares about most? Or will her burning need for freedom be the cause of their deaths?

FAMILIAR TERRITORY

CHAPTER ONE

The stupid cat was going to be the death of me.

He crouched beneath a rusted out cabinet and hissed whenever I moved. Every time I spoke to the bedraggled creature it spat at me and backed more deeply into the shadows underneath the cabinet. All I could see was the glow of his large green eyes. Beautiful eyes. Just about the only attractive thing about the ugly critter.

Including his personality.

"Come on, buddy. I promise I only want to help."

The cat yowled fervently, ending the long complaint with a hiss that promised me pain if I tried to get any closer.

I sighed my frustration, sitting back on my heels to think. I'd been chasing the recalcitrant feline for almost a week, and I'd been unable to lure it out with any of my usual tricks. The difficult creature had already snubbed kibble, tuna, even a can of delectable anchovies I'd dug out of the back of my pantry. I was at a loss. He didn't seem in the least inclined to let me "save" him.

I had only one last option and I was reluctant to use it. It was too easy and way too tempting. But it was starting to look like I wasn't going to have a choice.

Standing up, I quickly glanced around to make sure I wasn't being watched. The fenced in lot was empty except for me and the cat, and the street beyond the fence was quiet. Most of my neighbors were already at work, and the ones who weren't were probably still asleep.

The coast was clear.

But was my conscience?

I eyed the cat and earned another hiss for my trouble. That hiss twanged my last nerve. "Okay, fuzzface. That's it. You and I need to have a meeting of the minds."

The cat moved slightly forward as if drawn by my angry tones. I was surprised, but then the animal hadn't done anything I expected so far. It made a twisted kind of sense that he would continue to catch me off guard.

I gave it one more second's thought and then made my decision. The cat watched me as I walked to a spot several feet away and sat down, crossing my legs and spreading my hands on my knees.

The feline's intelligent green gaze was filled with antici-pation, as if he knew what I was about to do. I don't know how. Even I wasn't entirely sure if I was actually going through with it. I only knew I needed to do something or the cat underneath the cabinet would be lost.

So I closed my eyes and focused my thoughts inward, searching for the core of energy that pulsed in my breast. My tentative exploration was all too eagerly received. As I'd feared, the magic flared toward my tentative touch and grabbed hold, surging outward far too fast.

I panicked and clamped it down, gritting my teeth as the energy tried to break free. I barely managed to wrestle the magic back so I could control it. When I opened my eyes again I gave a yelp of surprise.

The cat was sitting right in front of me, its wide green eyes narrowed. I clasped my throat. "You scared me half to death." I smiled. "But I'm glad you showed up so I didn't need to use...well...you don't care about that, do you?"

The cat stared at me another moment and then, when I reached for it, growled and slashed at my hand, ripping several long slices across the back.

"Ow!"

He leapt into the air and took off. Before I could even move, the critter had scampered through the gate I'd apparently forgotten to latch, and disappeared.

"Dammit!" Jumping to my feet, I cradled my bleeding hand, briefly considering trying to go after him. But I couldn't even see the damnable creature anymore and I had no idea where to look.

"Are you all right?"

For the second time in moments I jumped in surprise. I swung around to find a tall man with dark, nearly black hair coming through the gate.

"I'm sorry to interrupt..." He swung his hands around as if to indicate the area. "...whatever you're doing here. But I heard you cry out." His dark silver gaze slid to my hand. "You're hurt."

I covered my hand and pulled my pride around me like a shield. "I'm fine." Starting toward the gate, I gave the sexy stranger a wide berth, determined to keep my distance. Unfortunately, he reached out and snagged my wrist before I could move past. Electricity surged between us, spitting from our fingertips and merging over our hands in a silvery-blue arc. A jagged volt of energy sliced through me, causing the magic at my core to flare painfully to life.

To my horror, my cheeks started to sting and my fingernails burned.

His gaze shot to mine and held. For just the briefest instant, I thought I saw something feral move through the silvery depths but it quickly slid away.

In a panic, I jerked away from his touch, all but running for the gate. He called out to me but I kept going. Whatever he was, I didn't like the way he'd affected me and I was going to make sure it never happened again. I didn't even slow until I reached the shabby, careworn brownstone I called home. Diving through the front door, I slammed it shut and locked it, leaning against the cool wood surface as I tried to calm my pounding heart.

What had just happened?

Had I really joined energy with a perfect stranger?

The implications made my stomach tighten with dread. Shaking my head, I pushed away from the door and hurried through the house to the sanctuary in the back. I'd lose myself in work...forget all about the husky-voiced hottie with the intense, silver gaze.

What had happened between us was just static electricity. Nothing more.

That was my story and I was going to cling to it with everything I had. Because the alternative was too terrifying to contemplate.

An hour later, as I was cleaning out a large kennel filled with soiled newspaper shreds and spilled food, my phone rang.

I pulled my cell from my pocket and looked at the ID, hitting the *Answer* button. "Hey, Mom."

"Peaches. How are you?"

Judging from the probing quality of her voice, I realized it wasn't a throwaway question. "I'm fine. Why?"

"It's just...well...I felt something a while ago. Something shifted in your universe."

Closing my eyes, I fought for calm, understanding that my mother, one of the strongest Familiars I knew, would hear any sign of stress in my tone. "I've been trying to catch this stray cat..."

"No. It's something else. What happened, LA?"

Biting back a groan, I tried again to throw her off the scent. "No really, this cat has really been stressing me out."

"LA, if that cat doesn't want to be caught you should respect its wishes. You of all people should understand that."

"I know, but it's so skinny and looks so sick. I'm really afraid it doesn't have long to live."

"You run a sanctuary, peaches, not a prison ward. Respect the cat's desire to die on its own terms."

She was right. I knew that. But it was killing me. "I know. You're right."

"Now tell me what really happened."

Sighing, I rubbed a hand over my eyes, suddenly oh so weary. "It was nothing."

"Trust me when I tell you it was something."

"The cat scratched me..."

"Yes?"

"And this guy asked me if I was all right."

Silence beat through the phone lines and I wanted to scream. She was doing exactly what I knew she'd do... assuming the encounter was important somehow. "It was just a guy."

"What happened between you?"

The woman was a Pitbull and she had my life firmly between her teeth, jerking fiercely. She wouldn't stop tugging until I told her what she wanted to hear. "He was just worried about my bleeding hand. That's all."

"LeeAnn Kristin Mapes..."

Oh gawd! Not the full name thing. "It was just static electricity!" I shouted into the phone in desperation.

Unfortunately there was no missing the huge gasp from the other end of the line. "You've found him!"

My head was shaking even before she finished the sentence. "I didn't find anybody..."

"You finally found your Witch, LA."

"I haven't found anything of the sort..."

"What does he look like? Is he handsome?"

I scrunched up my nose. "What difference does that make?"

"It makes no difference, but it doesn't hurt if he's cute."

Rolling my eyes, I looked down as a sleek black cat slipped along my calf. "He's very cute. Does that make you happy?"

"Oh, yes!" She actually giggled. I thought I might puke. "I have to call your grandmother."

Seeing a way out of the current conversation I eagerly agreed. "Okay, I'll talk to you lat..."

"Go see him right now and tell him you'll do it."

My eyes went wide. "Do *it?*" Good god, don't let my mother be telling me to have sex with a perfect stranger. My psyche would be permanently dented. I'd never recover.

"Offer your Familiar services. If he needs references let me know. I have a whole binder full of them."

"I don't even know if he's a Witch."

"When you touched, electricity arched between you, correct?"

I frowned, unwilling to verify the event for her. "Mom..."

"Your magic flared didn't it? You sprouted whiskers and claws?"

"No, I..."

"LA, stop denying reality. It's not healthy. And denying your birthright is even less healthy. Go talk to your Witch and make your blood pact. Now I have to speak to your grandmother. There are many plans to make. We'll have to have the joining ceremony at Grandmama's house. This place is under construction..."

"No, Mom..." But it was no use, I was suddenly talking to air as my mother disconnected, off to run my life for me since obviously I was unable to run it correctly myself.

If the doorbell hadn't rung in that moment I might have been able to sit down and figure out a way out of my predicament. But its insistent blaring through the brownstone was impossible to ignore.

And the person waiting for me on the other side was dangerous to my sanity.

Check out the entire series here: https://samcheever.com/books/#Reluctant

WHAT'S NEXT?

If you enjoyed **Nothing Familiar**, you might also enjoy these other fun mystery series by Sam. To find out more, visit the **BOOKS** page at www.samcheever.com:

Gainfully Employed Mysteries
Honeybun Heat Series
Silver Hills Cozy Mysteries
Country Cousin Mysteries
Yesterday's Paranormal Mysteries
Reluctant Familiar Paranormal Mysteries

ABOUT THE AUTHOR

USA Today and WSJ Bestselling Author Sam Cheever writes contemporary and paranormal mystery and suspense, creating stories that draw you in and keep you eagerly turning pages. Known for writing great characters, snappy dialogue, and unique and exhilarating stories, Sam is the award-winning author of 80+ books.

To learn more about Sam and her work, visit her at one of her online hotspots:
www.samcheever.com
samcheever@samcheever.com